NOTHINGHUMANLEFT

SI[illegible]N ASHE-BROWNE

Cargo Publishing (UK) Ltd
Reg. No. SC376700
www.cargopublishing.com

"Nothing Human Left"
Simon Ashe-Browne
ISBN-13 978-0-956308368
BIC Code-
FA Modern and contemporary fiction (post c. 1945)

CIP Record is available from the British Library

Cover designed by Craig Lamont 2011
Cover photograph by Neil Thomas-Douglas
www.neilthomasdouglas.com
Model: Michael Adams

First Published in the UK 2011
Published By Cargo Publishing
Printed and bound by
CPI Group (UK) Ltd, Croydon, CR0 4YY

ABOUT THE AUTHOR

Simon Ashe-Browne is a writer and actor based in Dublin. He was edicated at Gonzaga College and University College Dublin. He is a contributor to The Irish Catullus or One Gentleman of Verona, and in 2003, he was the overall winner of the Sean Dunne Young Writers Awards. Nothing Human Left is his first novel and won the 2011 Dundee International Book Prize.

1

Duke wipes the rain from the viewfinder and speaks into the microphone. "Soon he's going to explode," he says. "The earth will be scorched, and bodies mangled and charred within the blast radius." He zooms in on the back of the Doc's head, and lowers his voice: "And everyone will say, 'We should have seen it coming'."

The Doc stops, looks over his shoulder directly into the lens, and grins. His glasses glint in the lamplight.Then he strides on, pushing past a group of junkies sheltering under a portico. They melt out of his way. To Duke's way of thinking this shouldn't happen. No self-respecting scumbag should ever yield to a guy in a pink T-shirt bearing the logo "Work It". But even the scumbags know there is something supercharged about the Doc tonight.

With a quick shiver, Duke runs to catch up with his friend. As the camera closes in on Doc's lips, it catches him murmuring: "Work it, work it, work it."

"You not a bit cold?" Duke asks.

The Doc shoots him a dark look "Cold? Cold is for pussies." Then he ploughs through a puddle and swears at his feet. "Shit! My fucking boating shoes!" He stops for a moment, then raises his eyes imploringly at Duke. "I'm all moist," he says. "You know? Down be-*low*?"

Duke is cold and exhausted. "If it's all right with you," he says, putting the camcorder into his pocket, "I might go home".

"*Home*? You can't go *home*." The Doc grabs handfuls of Duke's coat. "Don't leave me, Dookey! Please. I need you." He pulls Duke eyeball to eyeball. "You," he hisses, "are my number one --"

"Your number one guy, I know," says Duke, prying Doc's hands from his duffle. "Okay, what about a drink?"

Doc charges off with his Terminator stride, glowing with renewed purpose, arms pumping like threshers.

They turn right at the end of O'Connell Street onto the quays, and arrive at the door of Zanzibar, which is being guarded by two bouncers; one with a skinhead, the other a mullet. As they make to enter, Doc is a poker-straight vision of confidence, while Duke radiates dejection. Doc gets the chest tip first.

"Not tonight lads," says the skinhead bouncer.

Duke covertly pulls the camcorder back out of his pocket. He's gotten pretty good at shooting from the navel in the past couple of days.

The Doc stares at the bouncer's fingers, then jerks out his hand so fast the bouncer balls his fist. "Hi there," he says, offering the bouncer a gentlemanly handshake. His voice is resonant with Harvard vowels, "The name's Bateman. I'm interested in patronising your fine establishment this evening."

The bouncer is inured to routines. "Not happening tonight, lads. Why don't yiz go home to your mammies? It's past your bedtimes."

"I can see you're a man of wit and sophistication," says the Doc. "But I'm afraid my mother perished recently. I consumed her this morning in refreshing smoothie form as an accompaniment to my bran muffin and all-natural yogurt." He rubs his stomach and smacks his lips. "A delightful repast!"

Skinhead bouncer takes a step forwards. "Take your act on the road, right?"

The Doc stands impassive.

Duke can sense what's coming.

When the bouncer is still a good three feet away, The Doc suddenly spasms and throws himself backwards. His feet go out from under him and he hits the pavement, hard.

Duke hears one of the smokers outside the club ask: "Did he get a smack?"

The Doc gathers himself slowly, his face a mask of grief. He stares down at his shaking hands.

Duke zooms in on the Doc's outturned palms, which, smeared with street dirt, look bloody and lacerated. Perfect shot.

"Why did you hit me, Daddy?" The Doc's voice is high and broken.

Duke pans out from the Doc to the bouncers. They wear the resentful smiles of audience members who can't decide if the stand-up comic is being a dick or if they're guilty of a sense of humour by-pass.

The Doc can see he has them on the ropes. "Why must you always hit me?" he whines. "Why must you always solve things with violence?"

"Now here-" says the skinhead bouncer.

The Doc jumps back, then bolts across the road between the traffic-jammed taxis, wailing pitifully, and dives headfirst over a wall.

The crowd collectively draws breath, waiting for the splash of the river. A girl in a too-tight black dress emits a short hysterical scream.

Duke trains the camera on the wall. He counts down into the microphone "Three, two, one, and–"

The Doc unfolds himself majestically on the far side of the wall, having landed on the boardwalk suspended over the Liffey. The girl who screamed looks momentarily embarrassed, then angry.

A rubbernecking clubber starts a cautious round of applause among the assembly. Doc stares back at them from across the road, resisting the urge to bow.

Duke pans from the Doc to the mullet bouncer and says sweetly: "You know, I don't think he really wanted to get into this shithole."

Mullet bouncer looks at Duke and then clocks the camcorder poking out from the folds of his coat. His disgusted realisation that the interaction is all on tape should make a great closing shot.

Duke hears the Doc shout "Bacon!" and turns to see him sprinting off towards O'Connell Bridge. Duke sprints after him and, entering into the spirit of things, squeals like a pig.

They jog together as far as College Green, the Doc suggesting between pants that they go find some hookers to make friends with. But when Doc takes his ease against some iron railings at Trinity College, Duke doesn't stop. "Good show tonight, Doc," he calls back to his friend.

The Doc swears after him, calling him a faggot, but Duke doesn't look back. It's time to go.

Tomorrow is, after all, he thinks, *a school day.*

2

But that's tomorrow. Halfway up Grafton Street Duke feels a guilty tingle between his shoulder blades. He checks the reflections in the unshuttered shop windows to make sure the Doc isn't playing the stalking game. The coast is clear.

He checks his phone and re-reads a text he received earlier tonight. *It isn't really a betrayal*, he tells himself, *it's just... hanging out with mutually exclusive friends.* The almost scientific neutrality of the phrase 'mutually exclusive' acts as a salve to his conscience. He keeps with his usual route home via Harcourt Street and the Charlemont flats but when he crosses the canal, rather than heading straight ahead to the village, he takes a left in the direction of Northbrook Road. He takes a shortcut though a park, keeping an eye out for axe murderers hiding in the bushes, keys himself into an apartment complex, and stands inside the gate looking up at the tastefully lambent citadel of Ranelagh Prospect Towers.

Up on the tenth floor is Bob's place; a gift from his tax exile father, one of the main financiers of Prospect Towers. Also up there will be Bob's retinue of druggie friends and hangers-on, mostly Xavier boys like Duke and Doc and Bob, with the occasional random hard case element thrown in to keep things lively.

Duke nods to the security guard at the front desk, who knows him by sight, and takes the elevator. The elevator is illuminated a sourceless blue glow. Above the twin rows of brushed steel buttons some genius has scribbled 'Podge was 'ere' (*correctly used apostrophes,* thinks Duke, *the private schoolboy give-away*). Below the buttons is another tag. In neat red marker, almost certainly inscribed by the Doc's fastidious fan-boy hand, is the first line of American Psycho:

Abandon all hope ye who enter here.

Duke takes his a pen from his inside pocket and writes below the Psycho quote; 'And this too has been one of the dark places of the earth'. He lets the sentiment settle, wonders if it's apt or pretentious or both, and decides it doesn't matter.

He gets out on ten, knocks on room 1003, and listens at the door. No sounds from within; no decks tonight. He knocks, waits, knocks again. Still nothing. While toying with the notion that being ignored might be a blessing, he hears clicks and the slide of a bolt from within. The door is opened a crack, revealing a long, goateed face. Chris. He stares at Duke as though he's never seen him before, then stomps off down the hall, flicking the door back as he goes, leaving Duke to catch it with his face if his hands aren't fast enough. Fortunately, they are.

What a terminally vicious cunt, thinks Duke, energised by a violent urge to grab him by his filth-stiffened ponytail and snap his neck, depressed by the recognition that he's not the sort of person who gives in to such urges. They enter the open plan living area, which looks like an IKEA showroom fashionably distressed by Pete Doherty. In one corner of the room a bin has overflowed like a landfill mountain, its lower slopes extending for a metre in every direction; a smashed panel of the French doors has been patched over with an extra large pizza box; rows of empty beer bottles line the walls.

Bob is sitting like a Pasha in his armchair, his lordly bulk filling out his shellsuit like a kaftan. He listens with a benign expression to Martins, who is in full flow, holding up scraps of paper on which he has concocted Miro-ish landscapes of bubbles and leaf shapes. Duke discerns the word 'fractals' over the drum and bass, and his eyes meet Bob's, who gives him a wanky aesthete look that Martins completely misses.

On a sofa the Boss is giggling hysterically at whatever is playing on the laptop of the pasty, porridge-skinned guy who always seems to turn up at these things. No one, apart from the Boss, knows who the pasty guy is or where he comes from but he's always there, creeping past you when you're going to the jacks, staring at you across crowded rooms with lightless eyes like sea washed marbles. Laura is curled up on the sofa under the window, binned out of it. Her grey trackies are riding low and showing off the soft tan of her lower back and a bright pink thong. Duke pushes the idiot longing out of his mind and decides he is equivocal on this matter; thankful for a glimpse of thong, but resentful that everyone else gets to see it too.

Balance is the key.

He hears a fleshy smack and a hiss of pain and looks into the kitchenette but it's just Chris and Houghton, playing punchy-facey.

Duke sits down in the only available seat, on the sofa beside the foetal Laura. He holds himself stiffly, making sure not to press against her. Then he reckons this might look like suspect behaviour and he relaxes into the old, brown upholstery, lets his legs splay, his left thigh unobtrusively grazing the curve of her bum.

There now, everything is groovy, sit in the chair like you just don't care.

He tries to focus on Martins' monologue, realises that all his attention is now focused on the contact between his thigh and Laura's bum and wonders, not for the first time, how it is that women do this. He gives himself a mental slap and crosses his legs. "Here, Duke, have a tinnie," says Bob, cutting across Martin's babble and indicating the coffee table, on which there are a few fresh cans among the ashtrays and empty bottles and discarded skins. Duke leans over and plucks an unopened Dutch from the mess.

"Jesus, Bob, that's a big block of brain damage you've got," says Duke.

In the centre of the coffee table is a brick-sized lump of hash.

"Yeah, Chris brought it over. We're doing a bit of business. Pretty special isn't it? Wanna try some?"

Bob proffers a joint, Martin's eyes following it like a lizard tracking a fly.

"Not really," says Duke, but he takes it anyway. "So. How's tricks, Bobby?"

"Good food and Class-A's man, good food and Class-A's. Living the life," says Bob, spreading his arms wide and taking in the surrounding decrepitude.

The thing is, thinks Duke, *this is the life.* For so many of his friends, pampered middle class kids every one of them, even the ones who dress and talk like scumbags, this is the dream, living like a junkie in notorious squalor, paid for by fat dads who don't care to know better, or just don't care.

And who am I to naysay it?

"Here, check this out," says Bob, picking up a small wooden box from the arm of his chair and holding it over the sleeping Laura, "and drag that or pass it."

Duke takes the box with one hand and a toke from the joint in his other hand. It's very strong and he has to suck back on a throat tickle to stifle a coughing fit. He flips the little brass catch and opens the lid. Inside is a very smooth, spherical, shiny turd. "Raw opium," says Bob, with the smile of a man who knows the score. "Chris smuggled it back from Amsterdam. Up his ass."

Duke snaps the lid shut and forces himself to swallow.
"Did he manage to fit this charming little box up his ass too? Seeing as he can squeeze his whole head up there."

Bob laughs. "I got the box from Mum's room. Wanted something nice to keep it in. I'm saving it for a special occasion. Interested?"

"I think I might pass on ass drugs."

"He had it in a condom."

"I'd say that fucker likes the idea of people eating his shit. We do it all the time anyway."

"Ah, he's alright."

"He's a cock."

"Yeah but, like, he's a good contact. Keep your voice down."

Chris is still in the kitchenette with Houghton, loudly proclaiming his genius as a drummer, completely oblivious to their conversation.

"He's one of the worst people I've ever met," says Duke, taking another drag. "He should be castrated."

The joint, though it smells and tastes strong, isn't doing anything, he's sure of it. He passes it to Martins, sitting on the floor hunched over a new doodle, who takes it eagerly.

"And how's the Doc?" asks Bob, pointedly.

"Same as ever. Only more so, recently."

"He's a fuckin' psycho," says Bob, with a rising, don't-say-I-didn't-warn-you inflection.

"No, he's not," says Duke, rolling his head against the back of the couch and turning over the thought. "I mean, he certainly wants everyone to think he's got psycho *capacities*. But it's all just *performance*."

"Well what about the fucked-up dog stuff?" says Bob.

The sanctimonious way he says this sparks off an explosive fit of the giggles in Duke.

Bob contrives to look offended and says, "It's not funny, Duke, it's fucking animal cruelty," but this only makes Duke laugh harder. Tears run down his hot red cheeks and he struggles to catch a breath to say, "Did I tell you about Doogie and the wind chimes?"

Bob shakes his head.

Duke breathes deeply to calm himself, and says, "It's partly my fault because I told the Doc about Pavlov one day and his face lit up like a pinball machine."

"On principle I don't find anything that guy does funny, but go on," says Bob.

"When Doogie wants to take a piss he paws the back door to be let out, right. So the Doc starts making Doogie wait to be let out, until he figures Doogie is bursting, and then when he does let him out he follows him with these wind chimes to Doogie's little leg lifting spot out in the back garden. Doogie starts pissing and then the Doc gives these wind chimes a belt. The Doc does this for three straight weeks, until Doogie's bladder release is completely tied to these wind chimes."

"You're making this up," says Bob.

"No, I'm not," says Duke, wondering for the first time if the Doc made it up. "Anyway, it's partly to annoy his dad, because his dad spent hundreds toilet training Doogie, but now if the Doc jingles these wind chimes the poor fucking dog starts pissing wherever he's standing with this befuddled expression on his face, while the Doc stands over him saying '*Baaad Doogie*'." He starts laughing again. Bob doesn't seem to get it.

"It's all about the befuddled expression," Duke says apologetically, trying to emulate that expression for Bob now.

"To be honest," says Bob, "I don't care what he gets up to with his dog, but I can't be arsed taking his shit anymore. Didja hear what he said to Laura?"

"No."

Duke feels the blood draining from his face, and the hash seizing control of his brain. A blast of paranoia sends his attention skittering to the far corners of the flat.

God I'm really stoned – no I'm not – yes I am. So very stoned. Any second now they'll cop it that I'm completely screwed and I won't be able to do anything about it – about what? – Why would they care anyway? I don't think they really do know; they're not paying any attention and why would they? Hold on, get a grip, Bobby talking –

"He said what?"

"He asked her if herself and Houghton had ever done anal. And, like, if they did, could he, y'know, join in next time. Pretty much. I mean that's fuckin' bang out of order, you can't deny it."

"It's just his sense of humour," says Duke with effort, scanning the floor, his head suddenly too heavy to lift, wondering if he can pass off this momentary slump as deep meditation on the matter. He realises that he doesn't want Laura to hear him defending the Doc. "The only ass he wants filled is his own," he says, flopping back into the cosy sofa, Freudian phraseology drifting past his mind's eye. "A typical anal-retentive," the words drawling out of him like soup.

God, it's like thinking through honey.

"Whaddya mean? He's gay?"

"No. Yeah. Maybe. I don't know. I just know, I mean I deduce from the available facts, that he holds that sphincter nice and tight," says Duke, clenching an illustrative fist.

"What d'you mean, 'anal-retentive'? He's got ass on the brain, like? He remembers asses? I don't get it," says Bob.

"Yeah," says Duke, raising his arms over his head in a gesture of hopeless incomprehension, "yeah, one of those," allowing a wave of giggles to pass through him. Bob joins in for the hell of it. Duke laughs to himself, and at himself, and at the Doc; *poor, stupid, hateful Doc, just what is your major malfunction?* He looks over at the Boss, still in hysterics at whatever's playing on the laptop. His face is beetroot red and wet with tears. The pasty guy remains blank as a toad. The Boss notices Duke looking at him curiously.

"It's this smurf porn," he says, spluttering, close to a heart attack. "There's a dog. He's... He's... doing her from behind. She's... She's wearing," he manages and then says in one breath, "She's wearing a little paper hat." He slaps his thighs, gasping. The pasty guy's eyes never move from the screen.

Duke manages a nod and a smile, to show he can appreciate the funny side of it. Chris shouts from the kitchenette and everyone freezes.

"Shut up you fuckin' muppets! We're listening to my beats."

Chris and Houghton stand side by side, sharing the headphones of an MP3 player, nodding their heads in unison, their expressions ferocious.

"It's this smurf porn," says the Boss, still laughing, but less loudly.

"What?" shouts Chris.

"Smurf porn, man," says the Boss, pointing to the laptop.

"Yeah, that's some funny shit," says Chris, not smiling.

My beats. What a cunt.

Something moves against his leg. Laura stirs, blinks down the length of herself and looks at Duke with slitty, sleepy eyes. Duke feels his own eyes, tiny inside a big balloon head.

"Hi," she says.

"Hi," he says.

"Can I have a little sip?"

"What?"

"Just a little sip," she says, plaintively smacking her dry lips. He realises he's still holding a can of beer.

"Oh yeah, sure," he says, passing it to her. She takes it, holds her head upright to take a few swallows and passes it back to him.

"Thank you, Dukey," she coos, still endearingly half-asleep. "You're always so nice to me. So nice."

"Oh well. It's not even my beer," he says, all modesty. He takes a draught down his own parched throat. She pushes against the cushions and sits up, cricking her neck and stretching out her wrists and arms as though unaccustomed to such long and delicate limbs. "I want a cigarette," she announces, fidgeting cans and lads mags around on the coffee table and finding an open pack. "You want one?"

"No thanks. My mouth's really dry."

"Go on, have a little cigarette," she says, holding it up before his eyes and rolling it between thumb and forefinger to prove how harmless it is.

"Naw, really, it's okay."

She sticks it in his mouth.

"There now," she says, taking one for herself, "everybody's happy. So, Dukey," she says, leaning close and lighting his cigarette, "What's. Up. With you?"

"Nothing much. Just hanging in there until I can get out of this dump."

"Bob's place?"

"No, Dublin."

She shakes her head, a half smile on her lips.

"Where you going to go? Australia? Everyone wants to go to Australia now."

"Nope. Australia's a cultural toilet. France maybe. I haven't decided. Just *away*."

"No special lady to keep you here?"

"Only you," he says, ironically but seriously.

"Aren't you the cutest. I'm sure there's loads of girls who want you."

"Alas, not the Irish girls. I know, I've tried and I've had it with Irish women."

"What's wrong with Irish girls?"

"They don't like me."

"You are a little freaky, I guess. Maybe you're a little too freaky for some Irish girls. I mean freaky in the good way."

"But of course. Whatever it is, they just don't want what the Duke's got."

"And what has the Duke got?"

"I have nothing to declare but my enormous penis."

She smirks indulgently.

"Naughty Dukey. Are you getting freaky with me now?"

Losing his boldness his eyes retreat from hers and he notices that the ash column of the cigarette he isn't smoking is now an inch long. As he reaches for an ashtray the column crumbles of its own accord. This carpet, he decides, can absorb another roll of ash. Laura's face is suddenly very close. She parts her lips.

"Push it in," she whispers.

He stares at her, paralyzed with bewilderment. She motions with her eyes to her left hand. The back of her palm is less than a centimetre from the burning tip of the cigarette he holds between index and middle fingers. The skin of her hand is pale and buttery. Duke does not often think in terms of sin, but he's certain that it would be a sin to mar that flawless hand. Laura pulls up the sleeve of her hoodie and shows him the inside of her forearm. There are a dozen or so raised pink scars, livid against the white skin and delicate blue veins.

"It's okay," she says softly, "I'm a cutter."

"Yeah, but..."

"Don't think about it, just do it. Quick."

He can't think. The hash is heavy in his system and all he can hear properly is the bass line of the Mezzanine track thumping in his brain. Feeling that he doesn't have a choice he presses his thumb against the butt of the cigarette and tips her skin with the burning cherry. She draws in a whistling cat's hiss breath.

"Stub it," she says.

He stubs it. The cigarette sinks into her, scrunches and fizzles. He pulls it away from the blackened hole and chucks it into the ashtray, waiting for the axe to fall. With her good hand she brushes away the larger flakes of ash and rotates the wound for him to admire. The hollow, right in the centre of her palm, between the fine bones connected to the knuckles, is pink and white and speckled with black motes. It glistens like hot wax. He pulls his attention from it and dares to look around the room, expecting to see Houghton glaring at him. But Houghton and Chris have their backs to him, still bobbing their heads to Chris' beats. Martins remains engrossed in his doodle and the pair of perverts on the sofa are still glued to the laptop. Only Bob meets his look. His eyebrows are quizzically raised and his lips curled with surprise and interest and mock disgust. But he just shrugs as if to say 'different rules apply' and goes back to rolling a fantastically complicated joint. Laura admires her burn, a dazed and almost spiritual expression on her face.

"I've asked Howie to do that but he's always been too pussy," she says, squeezing the skin around the burn. Duke regards her warily.

"Does it hurt much?" he says, unable to deal with anything else.

"At first, when you were just tickling it. But not when you stubbed. That felt good somehow. I think it'll sting in a minute, but it's worth it."

She glances at the kitchenette and gives Duke a peck on the cheek. Out of the corner of his eye he sees Bob mouthing the words 'Careful Now'. His awareness of the room comes back in a rush, like ears popping. The Boss is laughing noisily again, exclaiming to the room, "A poodle! A fuckin' poodle!"

"Here, I told youse muppets to SHUT THE FUCK UP!"

The room stops. Chris is pointing a silver, snub-nosed pistol at the Boss, who freezes mid-laugh. Martins looks at Chris with wide eyes, his pen suspended over the doodle. Bob's joint is in disarray on his broad lap. The pasty guy looks from the gun to the Boss's face with the same lack of expression Smurf porn had warranted.

"Here, Chris, chillax," says Houghton. "I can hear it fine." Houghton still has one earpiece in. The other dangles at his naval. The Boss's face has turned from red to white in the space of a breath. Chris stuffs the gun in the front of his pants.

"It's not even fuckin' loaded," he says scornfully.

"You're such a shithead, Chris," says Laura, alert and spiky but with one hand hidden under a cushion.

"That's a bit of a buzz-killer, man," ventures Bob.

"It was a fuckin' joke! Doesn't anyone get a fuckin' joke around here?" says Chris, swinging his humourless head at the room.

"That's a good one," says Duke, "You should tell it at parties." He stands up, fixes his duffle. "Catch you later, yeah?"

Everyone mumbles a goodbye except for Chris and the pasty guy.

"Hey," says Bob, "don't forget Julian's this Saturday. Should be a big one."

Duke nods ambivalently. He looks at Laura but she pretends not to notice. He leaves. On the walk home he keeps half an eye out for a lurking Doc. You could never be sure he wasn't out there. When he gets home and falls into bed his hash-hazed imagination performs erotic arabesques with smouldering skin.

3

The Doc stares after Duke until he can't make him out from all the other big wet coats on legs. He lounges against the black railings, his bare arms crooked around the posts, and wishes someone would take a photograph of him.

He searches the pockets of his rain stiffened jeans, just to make sure he's as strapped as he remembers. In the right pocket he has some loose change, less than a euro. In the left pocket is a wad of Monopoly money. He untangles himself from the railings and heads round the curve of Trinity College and up Nassau Street.
As he walks, he makes a point of eye-balling everyone he passes, and they all look away, which makes him feel good. Passing by Peggs he hears a long pealing cry of "Faggot!" A fattish, former-rugby playing type in a striped River Island shirt is staring at the Doc from the other side of the road. He lurches to-and-fro on the curb and shouts at the Doc again.

The Doc, on auto-pilot, turns to the wall. He grabs the railings above his head, spreads his legs and points his ass at the jock.

"You wanna come over an' fock me," he shouts back in a thick Cuban accent.

I am Tony Montana.

"You wanna piece-a sweet ass, beeg man? Come on over an' fock me!"

He traces a finger down the curve of one butt cheek, middle finger extending to the ring, booty shakes and then starts walking again. The fat guy mouths dumbly for a second and then shouts in a hideous mincing voice, "Love the shirt". The Doc dismisses him with a limp-wristed flick and keeps walking. Fitzwilliam Square is usually good for hookers, he thinks, but if not he could always carry on up to Burlington Street, by the hotel.

Where the fat cats go.

When he gets near Fitzwilliam Square he crosses the road and slows his pace. A woman is standing on the other side of the street. She stands in the shadow of the trees, leaning on one hip, wearing a shiny black puffa jacket, black skirt and black boots. He makes his way very slowly along the street, watching her out of the corner of his eye. She's thick-chested, and her black hair is cropped short and, to the Doc's way of thinking, dykey. Her eyes rest on him only once, and for less than a second, just long enough to dismiss him as potential threat or client.

The Doc walks on past her, then ten yards past the edge of the square, and sits on the stone steps in front of one of the Georgian office buildings.

Staking her out.

He sits there for a full five minutes and even though he's by far the pinkest and most eye-catching addition to the deserted street, she doesn't look his way again. She strolls up and down her side of the square a couple of times. He murmurs "work it, work it," but without much conviction.

A silver Mercedes S-class with cruises slowly past the Doc, heading towards the square. Doc stares at the driver, who stares back at him. The driver is a portly Irishman in a grey suit, with furtive, indistinct Irish eyes and jowls breaking softly over the crest of his shirt collar, but superimposed over the driver's face is the reflection of the Doc's; his bone white pallor, the slicked black hair, the level gaze behind the rectangular rims. In his own reflection he sees the image of Patrick Bateman he's been carrying around for years like a locket photograph of a beloved.

The Mercedes stops beside the prostitute. The Doc watches her lean down to the passenger side window. "Hey there, Big Boy," the Doc-as-prostitute whispers seductively.

Hi, says Pat.

"Nice ride."

This? This is a piece of shit. I only use it for cruising chunky pigs like you. Hah. I'm joking of course. You're a very attractive young lady. Would you like to get in? The seats are heated. Do you like whips?

The prostitute pulls back from the window and the Mercedes pulls off and goes left at the end of the square, out of sight. She follows it, talking into her mobile as she walks, and disappears round the corner. A minute later he sees the car driving off on the far side of the Square.

He gets up off the steps, his ass numb, and feels every muscle in his body straining against exhaustion. His body sends his brain a tentative suggestion that it might like to go home and lie down.

That's loser talk, he shoots back. *Losers go home, losers don't get the prime pussy, losers don't make the big bucks, losers won't make it in the City.*

He makes himself walk again. Up to Leeson Bridge, over the canal, past the Burlington Hotel. In the basement of the hotel, Annabel's nightclub, where that guy from the Doc's school was kicked to death, is dark and silent. Apparently they're making a movie about that guy now. Maybe the Doc could play him? Or maybe he'd be better as the guy who did the kicking?

He spies a swatch of purple, chiffony fabric snagged in a bush on the hotel side of the railings.

Lost by some rugger-bugger bird, he reasons, *blowing a jock in the bushes.*

He reaches through the railings and untangles it from the twigs. The swatch is only a couple of inches wide. It might be a scarf or a wrap from a dress, or a head-band or a shawl. At a loss he ties it half-Windsor style around his neck. Happy with his find he strolls round the corner onto Burlington Street. A hundred yards down the street is a girl. She is wearing almost exactly the same clothes as the hooker on the square, but her puffa is shorter and not shiny. This one is also, from a distance at least, attractive.

He strides towards her, trying to convince himself that his heart isn't pounding. She watches him coming toward her, eyes wide and wary. Five yards away and closing he sticks his hand out.

"Evening," he says, "Pat Bateman, at your service."

She scrutinises the outstretched hand without making a move, so he drops it.

"Please excuse my outlandish attire," he says in his clipped Bateman voice, "all my suits are at the dry-cleaners. Would you by any chance be a young mistress of the flesh?"

She cocks her head and gives him an I-don't-take-any-bullshit glare. He realises how young she is, no older than he. There are acne scabs on her chin. Her hair is lank and badly dyed. A little silver umbrella dangles by a hoop from one finger.

"Listen," he says in his normal voice, "Sorry. I don't mean to be a jerk."

Her eyes become a fraction less hostile.

His mouth moves silently, as he attempts to say something like -

I was just passing this way and I saw you, and I thought, you know, maybe, I don't know, I mean it's pretty cold out and I know I'm feeling it. The cold. And, maybe, if you wanted, you could come back to my place...

"You're very pretty," he says, and if his face wasn't frozen to his bones he'd blush at his own simpleton-speak.

"Aw, sweet," she says, advancing a step. Her voice is nicer than he thought it would be.

"But I don't take daddy's credit card, Pat," she says, up in his face, and a finger suddenly brushes his crotch.

His body spasms away before he can control himself. The touch of her finger sends a blast of images to his brain; he sees all the cocks she's ever seen, and held and sucked and taken inside her; and he sees his own cock, feels it as she must feel it, a tiny, icy nub of deadened flesh. *A joke.* He knows her coy little smile hides a smirk. He tenses and his eyes glaze over. He can actually feel something drop over his eyes, like a one-way lens – he can look out, but nobody can look in.

"Sorry Ma'am, plum forgot about the bishnesh end o'things," he says in a barker's drawl. "The name's J.C. Moneypenny, made ma fortune in trainsh. Big locamotivsh. Shteam, I told them and they said, Jay-Shee, you're a madman. So what'll it be doll-faysh, twenty?"

He has the Monopoly wad in his hand now and deftly pulls a yellow twenty from the roll, scrumples it up in his fist and flicks it in her face.

"Fifty?"

Same with a grey fifty.

"Here, stop acting the fuckin' prick!"

"How about a hun'red?"

The orange note bounces off her thin chest.

"Hell, let's raysh the shtakes, five hunnard an' I get to fuck you inny ass."

This time she swats away the pink five hundred before it hits her and a bubble of insults burst soundlessly in his ears. The girl is only inches from his face but it's like she's trapped in a fish tank, mouthing away in a vacuum.

This isn't how it's supposed to go.

He runs up Morehampton Road. On the trot he swings a kick at a plastic wheelie bin. It skitters a couple of feet but remains stubbornly upright.

Oh for the days of clanging metal garbage cans, he says to himself, though the days he so fondly remembers are not in his real life but in his movie life.

Up ahead is the hotel he and Dukey stole a fire extinguisher from earlier that night. He glances around for snooping cops but the street is deserted. He crosses the road and walks into the car-park of the hotel, nice and casual, thinking giddy thoughts about returning to the scene of the crime. The abandoned fire extinguisher pokes out, brazen and red, from the undergrowth of the prickly bushes where they'd stowed it. They made no effort to disguise it up so if anyone had been looking they would've found it easily enough. So maybe nothing had been noticed at all. The rain had washed most of the foam away. Trails and spoors of foam cling like old snow to the walls and drains of the service alley but the bulk is gone, and he experiences a pang of disappointment at the thought that perhaps no one had seen the beautiful white mound. It had been there, huge and bizarre. 'An explosion of art,' Duke had said, and no-one had seen it.

He walks into the empty space of the service entrance, arms outstretched, carving a Doc-shaped hole through the vanished foam. He twirls on the spot, flinging his scarf tie over his shoulder. The metal door in the corner is ajar. He stares brazenly at the CCTV camera bolted high up, and has a sense that no one is staring back. So he tries the door.

He claws his fingers around the rusted edge. He knows it's going to make a lot of noise when he opens it. He holds his breath and wrenches, gritting his teeth when the hinges squeal and pressing a foot against the bottom to soak up the deep metal humming. Then he goes in.

The corridor is illuminated by dim, blue sconces. He stands in the gloom, drenched in silence. Visible at one end of the corridor is a room, lit by the same blue light. The Doc can make out a small desk, like a schoolroom desk, and a chair. He skulks towards it, hugging the walls, out of his mind with fantastic terrors. At the doorway he takes a few shallow breaths to steady himself and pokes his head in. He snaps back. There is someone in the room, standing with their back to the wall, waiting for him. He expects a hand, a sound, some sort of movement. Nothing comes. An age of death horrors pass and, not knowing why, he looks round the doorway again. The person is still there, completely still, hands by his sides and the Doc realises it's just a boiler suit hanging from a peg on the wall. He stands up, breathing heavily.

He smoothes his hair back and looks around the room. On the table is a security guard's cap and a copy of *Nuts* magazine. At the far end of the room is a W.C. Something clicks in the Doc's mind; factors come together and present the only viable course of action. He looks back down the empty corridor, listens, but all is quiet. Then he takes the magazine from the table, listens again, and goes into the W.C.

He pats the walls for a switch and something grazes the back of his neck. He swats at whatever silent insect assailant is attacking him and his hand catches a thin nylon thread. He pulls, it clicks, and there is light.

Stealthily, ever so stealthily, he sits down on the lidless toilet, undoes his fly and turns the pages of the magazine with his free hand. The urine smell is old and cloying, and the twenty-five watt bulb turns his skin and the skin of the girls in the magazine the same dead-baby shade of pale. Neither circumstance bothers the Doc in the least. But none of the women are right. They're all too tit-heavy, too made-up and smiley and glossy. He sits there flicking through the magazine and giving himself an occasional experimental squeeze. Finally, in the back pages, nestled among the sex-line numbers and penis enhancement ads, he finds her.

She is on her hands and knees, staring straight at the camera under a byline that reads, 'Do me from behind and then cum on my ass, Call Me Now'. Her lips are parted and her eyes are wide, vacant and imploring, the eyelashes heavy with mascara. Skinny, blond, wearing a nipped in white blouse and a plaid school skirt, about sixteen, or at least she looks sixteen. She's perfect.

The Doc is back in Fitzwilliam Square, with the pretty hooker, only this time they're inside the fence, in amongst the trees. She has her hand on his crotch and he lets her unzip his fly and root around in his boxers. She looks into his eyes as she pulls his cock.

It takes some cajoling after that soaking, freezing, shrinking rain. He flags and he flops. He has to call her dirty names, slap her in the face a few times, finally turn her round and stick it in her ass while she screams that it's *Just Too BIG*. He has to focus. He has to concentrate. He really has to work it. But in the end, by God, he makes it.

4

The Doc walks the four miles home from the hotel, bleary-eyed and noodle legged, running on an empty scrotum. His legs threaten to buckle several times but he fights to retain his straight-backed posture – forever composing himself for the unseen audience.

At 4:46 am he turns the key in the lock of his front door. He opens the door with assassin stealth, holding the brass knocker fast against unwanted rattles, enters the dark hallway, and softly shuts the door behind him. In the hallway he listens for sounds of stirring. No movement upstairs. A familiar small scuffle in the kitchen, coming closer. Doogie's dirty white muzzle noses the kitchen door ajar and looks up at the Doc.

"Hello my lovely Doogie," whispers the Doc, soft and low as the sandman. "I can't play with you tonight, boy. Go off and sleep. Go on."

Doogie looks up at the Doc a moment longer and then withdraws his head. He does a slow, sad shuffle and then pads back to his basket by the Aga.

The Doc crab-steps over the creaky boards into the living room and plays one level of Quake with the sound turned off. As he works through the level, the polished glass panes of his dad's display cabinet tug at his attention. The panes frame the reflection of his face, illuminated by the TV glare. Eventually incapable of ignoring his own image he pauses the game and looks into the glass. He pulls joker faces with his widest smile and most maniacal brows, a series of tough guy poses with hard, slitty lips and eyes, pig faces, Chink faces, goober faces, zombie faces. He works his eyebrows separately from the rest of his features and incorporates different eyebrow arrangements into a sequence of gurns. He drops his jaw and stretches his mouth into a long 'o' of mute terror. By turning the TV on and then off and then on again the silently screaming face appears and then disappears and then reappears from the darkness. He lowers and raises the brightness level with the remote, and the face slowly gains intensity, seeming to come closer and closer out of a black pit. As the face becomes brighter and sharper he can almost hear the scream rising in pitch, until he worries that he might actually be screaming; his real voice becoming louder and louder as he holds the button on the remote.

Hey, Pat.

Hey.

What's the rumpus, Pat? You look a wreck.

Work hard, play hard, that's my whaddyoucallit, enigram, metagram...

Maxim?

Yeah.

What you get up to tonight?

Hit the clubs with my good friend Dookey. Drank many a fine beverage. Snorted coke off the shaven head of a Peruvian dwarf. Cute little fellah. Danced with many hard-bodied chicks, to the plangent strains of Phil Collins. Teased them with my sculpted pecs and rock hard abs for a while and bought cocktails for everyone. Charged everything to my gold Am Ex card. No big deal. The way the hardbodies pressed themselves against me I could tell they were hungry for my Rocket Cock. Its length and girth are legendary in fashionable circles. But I wasn't interested in clean chicks tonight. Waylaid on my nocturnal perambulations home by a cheap whore. Paid her handsomely for her degrading services in a public park. Too handsomely. She would have done it for free but you sometimes you have to give a little back. Civic duties and all that. I have to uphold my reputation as a respectable member of the wealth-generating classes. I understand the nobility of the philanthropic calling. My generous soul spurs me on.

So you really gave it to that cunt in the park?

She wanted it so I gave it to her.

But hold on there, Pat, isn't this just a crock of shit? Aren't you really just some loser kid?

Fuck you. Fuck off. Quiet time now.

The Doc jolts in his chair. The voice was suddenly so loud. He says quietly, to the empty air, "Even I don't think this is real".

I don't think you're real...

The Doc draws back his arm to fling the remote control at the cabinet. The thought of his dad coming downstairs makes him lower it.

He stares at the TV screen. Then he presses the red button on the remote and the room goes black. He rests his head against the back of the armchair and tells himself he'll go up to his room and climb into bed.

Any second now, he says to himself, and then his eyelids drop.

The Doc sees a man with oiled black hair, wearing a well-cut suit. It can only be Bateman. He tries calling to the man: Pat, hey, Pat. But there is no breath or power in his voice. The Doc knows that Bateman is going to change into something, something terrible, something the Doc has seen before but can't remember. He needs to see Bateman's face before it changes.

He feels a knife in his hand, like a butterfly knife or a switch-blade. His fingers work stupidly at the casing but he can't find a way to release the blade. He's right behind Bateman now and he walks around to see his face. But no matter where he stands he's always looking at the wrong side. He can see the oiled hair, the back of an ear, but no more. His only hope is to kill Bateman before he changes completely. But he can't make the knife work.

Very slowly, Bateman turns to face him.

The Doc runs.

He sprints between blocks of endless skyscrapers. In the reflection of his glasses he sees his pursuer. He is being chased by a huge, three-legged clown.

5

The Doc jolts awake. There is a long moment of queasy uncertainty about his identity, the inside of him indistinguishable from what he sees – this grey-light living room, these plastic and leather textures, all flat in the prevailing gloom, the not-quite-darkness before dawn. He rubs his face and his fingers meet the frame of his glasses, which explains the ache around his eyes.

The display cabinet with its polished panes has lost all of its sinister aspect from the previous night. His dad's model yachts line the shelves, their gilt masts and inlays dimly lustrous. The Doc's ashen, puffy face stares back at him, younger looking than it had seemed last night.

There's a racket coming from the kitchen, and he almost remembers something from his dream ... but it dissipates into tip-of-the-tongue names and stretched celluloid and then it's gone. He realises that his dad is putting crockery into the dishwasher with his usual fervour for making as much early morning clatter as possible. The grandfather clock reads twenty-five to eight. Breakfast must be sacrificed. The Doc knows that if he hasn't been discovered down here in the sitting room, and as yet there is no evidence to suggest that he has, Mr Feeley will assume that he's in bed and shout upstairs at him to get his ass in gear or he'll be walking to school. This is never an idle threat and the Doc does not feel up to an hour long walk this morning.

He peels himself out of the armchair, rainwater and sweat having formed a sticky bond with the leather. Tip-toe to the hall, quick glance to the kitchen door, which is closed, and then a stealthy ascent to the landing. Enormous relief that his bedroom door is shut fast. Commending himself on a masterstroke of deception, he opens and shuts his bedroom door with a loud bang. Then he sneaks to the bathroom.

The shower is so soothing he falls into a gentle, standing doze, and is only revived by his dad, on cue, shouting up the stairs. This sends him into scrambling overdrive to brush his teeth, get dressed, grab his briefcase, drain a glass of water and stuff a banana into his pocket. He squelches down the driveway in his waterlogged deck shoes, jumps in the passenger side and pulls the door closed. His dad reverses, at speed. The Doc mumbles an apology of a general nature, not daring to glance at his dad's profile, set like a marble frieze over rigid ten-to-two hands.

With the least obtrusive of movements the Doc knots his school tie in a full Windsor. His dad says, "Seatbelt," and again he performs the action with the utmost discretion, even stifling the click of the buckle as he presses it home. They turn into an estate of indenti-kit houses, and rally through a time saving rat run his dad claims to have pioneered, only to find it infested by every thieving bastard commuter in South County Dublin.

On the longest, straightest stretch his dad floors it. The turbo bites down and the Doc, a trifle worried, is shoved back into his seat. The speedo touches fifty-five as they pass a sign warning 'Slow – Children at Play'. Then his dad slams on the brakes and tenses his surging weight against the wheel.

The Doc's forehead smashes against the dash.

He bounces back into a seated position and his first thought to emerge through the pin-prick lights is that he should pretend that nothing strange or startling has just happened. His second thought is that it would be wise to refrain from rubbing his head or making sudden movements of any kind. He expects a rain of blows any second. They don't come.

The car idles in the middle of the road, slightly skew-ways. His dad speaks. "Where were you last night?"

"I was out with..."

"I'm not interested. I came downstairs this morning and I found you. *Whacked out* in the sitting room. Soaking wet. Wearing *unusual* garments."

"You mean my t-shirt-"

"Shut up. I'm talking now. When I stop talking you can talk. That's how dialogue works. You seem to have a problem with it. For whatever reason you continually fail to understand that when you are told to come home at a reasonable hour you should *be* home at a reasonable hour. Whatever about the way you choose to dress... I don't *care*... I don't particularly *care* where you go, who you're with, what you do there. Your... lifestyle choices are not of interest to me except insofar as they impact on *my* life. I *work*. I have a *job*. A very difficult and demanding job. As you are aware, or should be aware, I often have trouble sleeping. I especially have trouble sleeping when I have to sit up all night listening to your mother bitch and whine because you haven't come home. And if she's bitching and whining she doesn't sleep. And if she doesn't sleep, I don't sleep. And if I don't sleep I'm going to take it out on you. Am I communicating clearly?"

The Doc pauses long enough to make sure this isn't a rhetorical question.

"Yes."

"Good. Get your fucking act together."

Other commuters have been sidling around them during this speech. His dad gives the finger to a people-carrier full of rubber necking little girls in green uniforms. Then he puts the car in gear and powers off at a speed implying that, though he may have said his piece, he hasn't yet made his peace.

The Doc leans his head against the window and daydreams. Clowns and circus music and Doogies process through his mind as he absently unpeels his long-awaited breakfast banana. When his dad lowers the driver's side window the Doc bites back on a lame joke about it being chilly enough in here already. Without warning his dad smartly plucks the banana from his hand and flings it outside. The Doc watches it arc through the air, bounce off a tree trunk and skitter across frosty grass onto the pavement; his first potential meal since burger and chips after school the previous day.

"No eating in the car, Jonathon."

The banana looks so sad and lonely as they drive away from it and it recedes into a small yellow dot. For an awful second the Doc wonders if he might even shed a tear.

On the plus side, he thinks, *there's always the chance that someone might slip on it.*

6

As Duke descends the stairs he senses activity in the kitchen. He goes into the living room, which opens onto the kitchen, and stops just inside the door.

"Is that you, darling?"

Duke is obscured from view of anyone in the kitchen by a half-wall. He hears the crackle of the frying pan. Whatever is being fried smells buttery and delicious.

"Darling?"

Am I hiding? Why am I hiding?

"Morning," he says.

He walks into the kitchen, straining to be unobtrusive.

"I'm making pancakes," says his beautiful mother and she gives him a brilliant smile. She is wearing a white bathrobe, white socks and a subtle trace of last night's make-up.

"I'm only having cereal," he says, his voice flat and almost spookily stripped of affect or affection, even to his own ears. The statement, as expected, is ignored. A plate of pancakes is plonked on the table at his usual place. The pancakes are light, saucer-sized, each a centimetre thick and plainly, irreproachably delicious. Already set out on the table is a bottle of maple syrup, a bowl of strawberries and blueberries, butter, whipped cream and a motley of preserves.

Resistance is futile.

He sits.

"Where do you learn this, mum?" The words emerge stillborn, cling-wrapped in cynicism. "Is there a book about this somewhere in the house? This can't be natural behaviour. Don't tell me you've been reading Nigella Lawson again?"

His mother scoops two pancakes onto a plate and pours two more exquisite discs of batter on the pan.

"Who are you even cooking for?" he says, blobbing cream and strawberries on top of his stack.

"Gregg and I are going to Maeve's opening tonight if you'd like to come. I know she'd love to see you there."

"Maeve... Maeve... curly white hair? Can't ever find her 'cunt-ing glasses'?"

"That's Fiona. *Maeve*. You know Maeve."

"Mum, I don't know Maeve. I rarely have any idea who you're talking about."

"Maeve did the series of passionflower prints. You liked them. I remember you said something about them, she was very impressed, she wrote it down actually... "

"That's you. You did the series of passionflower prints."

"No..."

"You're projecting aspects of yourself onto other well-preserved society dames again."

"No, darling, I did the *magnolias*. Maeve did passionflowers."

"Aha, all becomes clear. Some sort of horticultural agon in paint, is it? And I, no doubt, am just another pawn in the match for supremacy?"

She flips a pancake.

"I can't have any part in these demented parlour games," says Duke. "I'm probably going out with the Doc tonight. Or not. I don't know."

"Well maybe you and the Doc can stop into the gallery before you go out. There'll be plenty of free wine."

"I know there'll be plenty of free wine."

The French doors open and Gregg comes in, swaddled in a heavy coat and scarf.

"Hey-hey," he says to Duke, waggling his eyebrows. Gregg walks behind Duke's mother and pats her just above the bum, a gesture Duke is convinced is a taunting compromise made for his benefit. The gesture says, *I'll take a proper handful when you're not looking.* Gregg gives her a peck on the cheek.

She giggles and swats him away. "Your bristles are like icicles, Gregg," she says.

He strokes his beard, snow white against tanned Californian skin. "S'cold out. Pancakes smell good. How you doin' buddy?" he says to Duke.

"Fine. Good."

Apart from the fact that you're fucking my mother.

"How's the writing den coming along, Gregg?" she says.

"It's lookin' good. Might need some proper insulation in the roof. I'm thinking of getting one of those little wood-pellet stoves..."

This must be a joke.

"...but I might leave it 'til next year," says Gregg.

Oh, next year. Sticking around, are you?

"By the time I'm done the weather should be picking up anyway."

Looks like it's going to be a long cold winter to me, Gregg.

"Actually I was wondering about getting a wood-pellet stove for in here," says Duke's mother.

"Really, mum?" says Duke. "And where in this tiny house are you going to squeeze yet another bulky peaon to bourgeois rusticity? Between the oversized farmhouse cupboard thingy and the bog oak wine-rack?"

"I hear they're quite economical..."

"On top of the replica Aga?"

"...but really I'd just like to have a real fire in the kitchen."

"Why not just take out my bed and put the stove my room? I'll curl up beneath it and make non-confrontational purring noises. Seriously, the last thing this cosy love-shack needs is another superfluous heat generator."

"Getting a bit hot under the collar yourself there, buddy," says Gregg.

Duke finds himself unwilling or unable to meet Gregg's eyes. He knows they will be mercilessly all-seeing above the genial beard. Duke has been pinned by this look before. The look says, 'I know this is difficult. I know you're unhappy. But I love her too. Now deal with it. Or I might have to drop the down-home corn-ball and make it clear that I am a man and you, as yet, are not'.

Duke concentrates on swallowing his breakfast. It's time to go. As he skirts round the table to get to the door, still avoiding Gregg's eyes, his mother calls after him, "There's a letter for you on the hall table!" He tries to inject some free-wheeling bonhomie into his parting, "Thanks, mum." It doesn't come out right.

Duke pulls the front door of his house behind him, waggles the letter, and breathes in a morning of blue skies and hoarfrost. The letter is unexpected, and the crisp glory of the day is unexpected, and in the moment of unlatching the gate his morning doldrums unexpectedly evaporate. He says to himself,

I don't have to go right when I open the gate. And I don't have to carry on up Beechwood Avenue and past the houses I don't even see and by the church and through the back-gate and into room 6 to take notes on the fisheries dependant economy of Norway. I don't actually have to suffer the boredom of a day like any other day. I could pretend to be a free man and go left instead.

So he does, his eyes opened and his limbs revived by the elixir of truancy.

At the café on the corner he joins a queue of stressed-out suits and picks up a large black coffee. Being a man of leisure among the ranks of the harried perks him up even more. Before leaving the cafe he removes his school tie and buttons his duffle coat all the way to the neck to hide his school jumper. Then he doubles back off the main Ranelagh road in case a teacher spots him and chooses a route to Belgrave Square that will be less thronged with pedestrians. At the Beechwood junction of the LUAS line he rummages for some small change.

He examines the letter while chewing a pellet of gum. The white envelope has been doctored so thoroughly he's surprised there's no tell-tale strip of tape.

Postal authorities must be getting lax in the Christmas rush...

The return address reads 'Patrick Bateman, Crystal Sky Palace, The City '. Beneath it is a sketch of the Doogie being subjected to some form of cartoon torture. The Doc is a poor draughtsman and the exact nature of the rendering is somewhat obscure. Doogie is skewed through the anus by a shaft of some kind, that much is clear.

But is this simple canine buggery or something more? Is Doogie's bloated appearance intentional? Does the poor pooch's ballooning torso indicate that the shaft is in fact a hose-pipe? Should the Doc's obsession with the penetration, irrigation and general defilement of asses both human and bestial be considered pathological?

The envelope is artfully dotted with what Duke can only hope is the Doc's blood, sprayed as though he'd dipped a toothbrush in a puddle of gore and run his finger along the bristles. Nestling in one corner, small and light enough to have escaped his attention at first, is a flattish, oblong lump. It feels like hash but the Doc never smokes, nor is he in the habit of giving away luxury items.

Duke sticks a five cent to a one cent with his gum and places them in the groove of the tracks for the LUAS to squash together. He notices a little boy across the tracks watching his deviant activity with acute interest.

The tram glides into the station and Duke hears the little clicks as the metal wheels roll over the coins. He steps back to allow commuters to get into and out of the carriage. The LUAS pulls out of the station.

Duke picks up the squashed copper oblong, the one cent embedded nearly flush in the stretched five cent, and rubs off wispy strands of chewing gum. He crosses the line and offers it wordlessly to the little boy. After a moment of dark scrutiny the boy accepts it with chubby fingers. Duke smiles at his mother. In a tense sighing voice, good middle-class breeding stifling her desire to tell Duke to fuck off and stop corrupting her child, she says, "Say thank you to the man." The boy nods and makes a noise in his throat, agreeing with his mum if not quite willing to articulate a thank you. Duke mimics back the throat-noise and then walks off, wondering when he started looking like 'the man'.

Belgrave Square is hazy and beautiful.

Duke chooses a bench where he can sit with his back to the sun and watch the mist ghosting over the grass. He draws out the dull silver letter opener from the pen holster in his bag and splits the top crease of the envelope, takes out the two pages of the letter and lays them aside to examine the curious object lurking in the corner. The lump is brown and sweaty looking. He gives it a tentative stab with the letter opener, impales it and brings it up to his eyes for closer inspection. The colour and striations could be indicative of wood or… meat.

A sliver of meat.

A quick sniff confirms three to four day gaminess. It was an impressively considered move on the Doc's part to mount a surprise meat attack on a vegetarian. Though Duke would usually endeavour to keep the paraphernalia of a letter together he flicks the sliver onto the grass, overcoming the smart to his sense of clerical completion. He takes a sip of his coffee and unfolds the letter. The first page (helpfully titled 'Page One') is densely inscribed back and front in tiny, robotic script.

Dookey!

Do you like your present? It's a labia I bit of a whores vagina - obviousley - a shisem of flesh for your perusal - you sicko - how am I? O, thank's for asking, I'm fine, just dandy, not really, I'm feeling pretty twisted to be honest, turn to page two for my updated list of complaints and aggrevences - heres a story I wrote just for you - The business man drove through the City one dark and lonly night - his Rocket Cock burned in his skintight CK boxers beneath the $2000 raw silk Versace suit - he picked up a hitchhiker by the side of the road, her nipple's hard little nuts from the freezzing rain, poking through the wet fabric of her Gap top - he lashed her with duct tape to a black bamboo chair he'd picked up from the sales at Barneys in the living room of his penthouse apartment with it's view of the West side of the park and the glittering skyline – he records her screams on his new Sony digital Dictaphone so he could listen to them later when her throat gave up – then he placed an order for Chinese food, double chilli black bean beef with noodles and won-ton soup and it was delivered by a slanty Chink delivery boy with bad yellow teeth – the business man was revolted by the teeth and refused to tip the Chink delivery boy until he promised to invest in bicarbonate of soda – he ate in a room he hadn't ever been in before which looked like all the other rooms in the apartment – as he grappled with a slipperey prehensile noodle he was suddenly overcome by a nameless dread – he thought he was going to die and then he found a Dictaphone in his pocket and played it back and heard screams and picked up the carton of won-ton soup and threw it at the wall and then threw the black bean beef and the noodles – the noodles stuck to the sauce and slid down like slow-moving worms and he vomited up everything in his stomach – he got down on his hands and knees and drew pictures of headless women in the pats of vomit – the next day he has to go to Singapore on business – he returns to the apartment a week later – when he opens the door the stench hits him like a cloud of flies – the Chinese food is still plastered to the walls and fungus sprouts from the deep shag-pile carpet and maggots rithe in the beef bits – its all so disgusting he moves to his sisters across town and calls in a industrial cleaning service – they do an excellent job and he makes a point of recommending them to everyone at the office.

Page two is shorter. The letters are pressed into the paper as though written with a full fist.

The Death List (Renewmented)

Houghton
Laura
Bob
Matthews
Fleming
Dookey (I jest, ho-ho, ha-ha, hee-hee, I'm such a kidder)

P.S. The Clown's back.

Duke folds the letter neatly back into its envelope. 'Renewmented' is a good Doc neologism. And 'slipperey prehensile noodle' is nicely redolent of William Burroughs, even if it doesn't make literal sense. He feels a little swelling of pride that he's had so much influence on the Doc's style. Back in third year Duke took charge of the Doc's reading habits, introducing him to the Beats and Hunter S Thompson and – perhaps regrettably – *American Psycho.* He can even claim to have been indirectly responsible for the Doc becoming 'the Doc', given that an episode from *Naked Lunch* had inspired one of his most infamous performances.

It happened during an unsupervised science period and Duke can vividly remember the communal realisation that no adults were going to intrude on the class, and the concomitant feeling that there was practically a duty to misbehave. He remembers the Doc – who was only ever John or Jonathon back then – getting up from his chair and testing the door of the strictly off-limits supply room, finding it unlocked, and slipping inside. Minutes later, he emerged wearing a white lab coat and plastic goggles, carrying a plastic crate filled with preserved rats and frogs and an enormous rubbery cow's heart. He plonked down the mass of dissection materials on the absent teacher's desk, glared at everyone through the goggles, and said, "Nurse, fetch me a scalpel please. I have to surgerate on these animals. They look sick." Duke complied.

The Doc started by cutting open a rat and trying to massage what he thought was the heart back to life while quoting scraps of dialogue from Naked Lunch, but he soon ran out of material and had to invent his own riff, which involved constructing a chimerical beast from all the available dead animals and attempting to reanimate it. Duke played Igor to the Doc's mad scientist, lurching in and out of the supply closet to gather scalpels and retort stands and bottles of ammonia while the Doc hacked away at the bodies and screamed, "We can't lose this one, Dukey!" They tied a daisy chain of frogs around the cow's heart and stuffed rats' tails into the gaping aorta as the stench of formaldehyde and butchers block filled the room and the rest of the class pounded their desks like tribal drums. When the ball of bodies was sufficiently augmented, the Doc ripped the cable out of an old desk lamp and demanded of the class, "Do you want to see it LIVE?!"

The class pounded their desks and chanted, "Live! Live! Live!"

The Doc pierced the cow's heart with a metal skewer and his eyes flashed towards Duke for a fraction of a second, "Plug it in," He commanded. He threw his head back and cackled – to give himself courage, Duke could see – and touched the cable against the skewer.

The Doc christened himself that day among enraptured applause and an explosion of smouldering frogs. But that was then and this was now. Duke puts the letter in his bag and heads for Xavier.

7

The Doc joins the streams of green and grey and maroon jumpers as they swarm into the foyer of the school. His laminated, credit card size timetable, of his own meticulous design, tells him he is to go to room 8.

Every school has at least one narrow, bottle-neck corridor down which it is customary to receive a daily hazing until you reach the upper years. Being a sixth year the Doc is normally immune to kicks, shoves, thumps or trips. The fifth years and other sixth years consider it beneath them to engage in corridor malarkey, and first, second and third years are too small and scared to try anything on the older boys. Only the perpetually bored and fidgety fourth year posed a threat. By an unfortunate timetabling coincidence all three fourth year classes are booked into facing rooms of the corridor for the first period on Fridays. Sixty-odd of the shifty malcontents are slumped against the walls in tunnel formation.

Preceding the Doc into the corridor are three tiny first years, padding softly and silently over the fourth years' outstretched, trip-wire legs. The fourth years appear to be somnolent, but they are watchful as crocodiles. The Doc doesn't rate the chances of the first year in front of him, the last and littlest of the trio, bent double by a school-bag half as big as himself.

Sure enough he gets the first trip. He half-trots over and away from it, straight into a volley of kicks from the other wall. The other two abandon their cautious progress and sprint through a miasma of flailing legs. The little guy tries to follow them but a full-foot connection with his bag sends him into a crashing spin onto a row of fourth years. They push him upright and he stumbles back into a fresh offensive of Doobs, Clarks and Nikes, which kick him clear.

The Doc notes with disgust that the little drama queen is having the time of his life. He launches himself spread-eagled against a wall and then bounces theatrically to the floor. His bag props him up like the shell of a beetle as he pedals the air. Joy bubbles out of him as he rubs phantom pains, joy at receiving a beating from the older boys.

Legs are drawn back as the Doc enters the tunnel. He walks slowly and deliberately between the ranks, his briefcase and business-like demeanour a familiar and irreproachable sight as he silently dares them to try it on. One dozy, lank-haired fourth year neglects to retract his excessive limbs. The Doc stops in front of the offending legs, the tips of his boating shoes grazing fourth year's trousers. He looks from the legs to the face.

"Excuse me," he says, "Do you have a problem with the progress of the working man?"

"Wha'?"

"Are you deliberately impeding my progress?"

"Fuck off. Faggih."

The Doc's lips tighten. His brow furrows over black-rimmed glasses.

"I see no reason for upbraidment of my sexual character."

"You're a fuckin' homo."

In a single smooth movement the Doc drops his briefcase on the fourth year's shins and throws his full weight into a savage kick.

He connects with a chicken chest sternum, picturing his foot going straight through the skinny torso.

The fourth year wraps himself in his arms. He squints up the barrel of the Doc's accusatory finger, into the hollow staring eyes.

"Get a job, hippy. I don't like your negative attitude."

Smoothing back his already perfectly smooth executive do, the Doc walks up the corridor and joins his classmates outside room 8.

Mr Carey, bald, bespectacled and self-consciously classical in manner, is in a relaxed and freely extemporising mode. Feet crossed on his desk, he addresses the view beyond the window, like everyone else in the school, counting down the minutes to the end of the last day of term.

"In many ways," he declaims in his disinterested, nasal tones, "in many ways the 1916 Proclamation of the Irish Republic was a startlingly egalitarian document – much more so than the Constitutions which followed it. Significantly the Proclamation guarantees religious liberty, equal rights and equal opportunities to all its citizens. Cribbed from the French and no bad thing..."

The Doc, slipping further from self-consciousness with each passing minute, is daydreaming. Feet jigging beneath his desk, he silently addresses the back of Carl Deegan's skull, and imagines it being split with an axe.

"...despite invoking the protection of The Most High God, no special mention or provision is made for the Catholic Church. The idealistic fingerprints of Padraig Pearse are all over the Proclamation of course, couched as it is in his signature high flown rhetoric...

Splitty-splitty, chop-chop, bone-smashy, blood-splatty brains all over the floor.

"It is my belief that the ideals of liberty, equality and fraternity as they are propounded on the page would not have found manifest expression in the State, should Pearse somehow have escaped execution after the Rising and established himself as a political leader. Bit of a dreamer, I've always thought. Not quite connected to the real world. You have one of his noble sacrifice poems there on page 134. Mr Connaughton, do us the honours."

Red all over the window-pane, red light in the room, Carey screaming, running like a girl. Chop off their heads, chop off their heads!

"... to break their strength and die, they and a few," reads Paul Connaughton, "In bloody protest for a glorious thing."

"Thank you Mr Connaughton, that'll do. All very bloodthirsty and heroic stuff. But despite the ferocity of his verse Pearse, we know, was horrified by the reality of violence. He was hit especially hard by the civilian casualties in '16, of which there were a great many, almost double the losses of rebel and British forces combined. His poetic nature conceived of violence as not only necessary to the cause but as something virtuous and noble. But the fantasies of heroism that sustained him were shattered by this 'confrontation with the real'. Witnessing the suffering of innocent people on the streets was probably the main reason for his surrender. Mr Feely you look perplexed."

The Doc's brain scrambles for a playback of what Mr Carey has been talking about.

"No sir. I was just thinking. About Pearse."

"Would you care to share your august reflections with the class?"

"Not really, sir."

"Share them anyway."

"Eh, well, I was just thinking about the way Pearse thought about blood and killing all the time and how that was, y'know... great. But, when it came down to it, he was sort of a coward. Like you said."

"Well thank you for your penetrating insight, Mr Feely, though that wasn't exactly the point I was endeavouring to make.

Is there something else?"

"Yeah actually," says the Doc, improvising wildly with the day's photocopied hand-out. "Just a point of clarification. You see here in the Proclamation, last paragraph, ehh, yeah – 'We place the cause,' blahdiblah, emm, 'and we pray that no-one who serves that cause will dishonour it with cowardice, inhumanity or rapine.' You see just that sentence there?"

"Yes?"

"Yeah, I was just wondering, emm, is 'rapine,' like, rape?"

"Yes it is, Mr Feely."

Steve has already siphoned off the ether by the time the Doc gets to Biology.

Since Fitzer (one of Xavier's many resident drug-lorists) had discovered big glass jugs of the stuff in the lab, he'd inducted a faithful few into the instant-drunk pleasures of sniffing ether. Steve is the most devoted acolyte. He sits at the back of the class-room beside Fitzer, perched unsteadily on his high stool, red-faced and giggling. As the Doc approaches Steve dips his head below the level of the counter-top. His back rises and falls and he straightens up in his seat, breathing deeply, eyes rolled back in their sockets.

"Whatcha got there, Stevie?"

Steve convulses with high-pitched laughter. Fitzer smiles his cat's-cream smile and points with his foot to a towel on the floor between their stools.

"We soaked it in ether," says Fitzer. "Finished off the jug. There's only this much left."

He holds up a plastic Evian bottle which is full to the brim. Steve's face deepens in colour.

"Whatever you do," says Steve, his head lolling back and forth on his elasticated neck, "don't light a match."

The air around them is clammy with fumes. Steve, practically crying, says, "I think my brain is going to bubble out my nose!" Then he bends back down into the haze of eye-burning vapours. The Doc produces his hanky, a filthy, snot-stiff mainstay.

"Any medicine for the Doctor?"

"Yeah, sure," says Fitzer, "just don't, y'know, wipe the top with that thing."

Without dropping eye contact with Fitzer the Doc unscrews the cap of the Evian bottle, clamps his hanky over the opening and tips out a shot. All innocence, he looks down at the bottle.

"Oops. I made a boo-boo."

"You're *such*. A *cock*."

The Doc plonks the ether bottle on the counter and goes to the front of the class to take his usual seat. He presses the rag against his nostrils and sucks huge draughts direct to his brain. It hits him instantly. His heart starts pounding rabbit fast and his limbs lose all strength, flopping elastically as his brain tries to balloon out of his skull. The pressure builds inside his pumpkin sized head, squeezing his eyes into piggy holes.

Mr Kelgin strides in, clipped and pressed. "Be quiet," he says automatically. Steve stifles his giggles as best he can. The other twenty odd students cease their conversations or else, like the Doc, though not for the same reasons as the Doc, aren't saying anything anyway. The Doc just about manages to slide the ether sodden hanky into his lap and out of sight.

"We were looking at bacteria. Page 176," says Mr Kelgin, all business. The Doc has no biology book. His briefcase contains no text books at all.

"Mark. Hey Mark!" he whispers to the tall, blond boy a few feet up the counter. Mark either doesn't or pretends not to hear him. "Mark! I need to look in with you!"

Mark is definitely ignoring him.

"Mark! Share your book with me! Friends share, Mark! Don't make me come over there."

"What is the matter, Feely?" says Mr Kelgin.

"I'm sorry sir. I don't have my book with me. I was hoping I could look in with Mark, sir."

"Then do so and stop annoying me."

"Thank you, sir."

The Doc turns to Mark and pats the stool next to his own. Mark, after a moment of internal wrangling, gets up from his place and sits where he has been bidden. He slaps the book between them.

"Thanks, Mark. You're a real champ."

The Doc drops his nose an inch from the pages of the book, completely blocking Mark's view.

"Here, Feely. Move your head. I can't see. Move your head, Feely!"

But the Doc's attention has been caught by something in the biology book. He pulls it closer so he can focus his ether-shot eyes and read the passage.

"Here, Feely..."

"Shush, Mark."

"Feely, you're getting blood all over my book."

The Doc looks at the fascinating blob of red on the page. Another blob lands beside it. And then another. He touches a finger to his upper lip and feels the warm wet blood gathering from his pumping nose and he realises that the ether snorting must have burst a vessel.

"Yeah," he says, "so I am."

He giggles and shakes his head over the page, dropping constellations of blood spots all over the article on bacteria. He licks his lips and shows his vampire teeth to a disgusted Mark, who shrinks away.

"Better hope I'm not catching," he says, smudging the blood with the heel of his hand. Then he asks Mr Kelgin if he can be excused.

First a thorough preliminary lather, requiring three measures from the soap dispenser. He allows the unguent to soak in and work its cleansing action on the germs he can actually *feel* swarming about on his skin. Then a burning hot scrub, followed by another shot of soap and a quick lather, concluding with a prolonged cool rinse. Four shakes, no patting, and he's about to turn to the hand-dryer when something catches his eye in the mirror.

He presses the tap release again and holds his hands under the water, sluicing the water round the bowl while keeping an eye on the cubicles in the mirror. He half knows that he's half trying to scare himself. But he also has a mental image of someone watching him through a crack in the door of one of the cubicles. It's only the vaguest impression of a face, a very white face, and that disconcerting feeling of an eye meeting his eye and imparting a message he doesn't understand. He turns to the bank of cubicles and says "Hey!" in a voice that surprises him by its timidity. The resounding silence pops in his ears and then the bell for the end of class rings and he almost screams.

He feels dizzy on his way to Classics. As he walks among all the scurrying schoolboys he imagines cutting them down with laser beams shooting from his fingertips. People are so defenceless and unwary. They never held themselves in readiness against the cataclysm that might come at any moment.

Against me.

A thin, bespectacled third year hurries in frenetically uncoordinated style along the corridor towards the Doc, his tiny boys head cartoonishly wrong with such elongated limbs and barge-like feet. Out of sheer curiosity the Doc waits until the third year passes on his inside and then shoulders him into the heavy wooden lockers.

The boy bounces into them, smacking his forehead, but he keeps running, throwing a backward glance at the Doc. His mouth moves but he utters no audible retort. The Doc, dizzy and detached, watches him go, feeling like he's discovered a New Thing. He whistles the circus theme as he walks to biology, happy as a clown.

Doo-doo-doodle-oodle-uh, doo-doo-doo, doo-doo-doodle-oodle-uh-doo, doo- doo-doo...

"Now there was really no reason not to get one hundred percent in this test," says Mrs Moriarty as she hands back exam papers. "This was easy material – well done, Dara. If you don't know the basic chronology and events of the Iliad by now you'll have a tough time of it next year – you lost that ten percent because your handwriting is atrocious, Mark, absolutely atrocious, no Leaving Cert examiner would take the time to interpret that scrawl and if you think otherwise you're... well, you're in for a nasty surprise."

She releases the Doc's paper as though it is soiled. The document is marked at the bottom with a large red 20%, circled, with an exclamation mark. The Doc absorbs her overly rehearsed 'withering stare' without blinking.

"Why do I even bother, Mr Feely? Why do you even bother turning up? Why must we waste each other's time?"

"But Miss, I'm eager to learn. I love Classics."

"Don't take that *facetious* tone."

"I'm not being facetious, Miss. I don't even know what facetious means really. Classics is my favourite subject. It's numero uno. I mean, I just can't understand what's going wrong. Is it me? Is it you? It's so hard to say..."

"Would you like me to tell you what's going wrong?"

"I'm all ears, Miss."

"You're lazy. You're disruptive. You impede yourself but more importantly you impede other students' *learning*. We get dragged into these pointless discussions every class and I'm, frankly, not even going to do it this time, there's absolutely no point..."

"But why would I do that Miss? Why would I want to disrupt the *learning environment*? We have to ask ourselves the question; is there any chance you're just a terrible teacher?"

She freezes. The brazen insult squats between them like a smouldering firework.

"Get out," she says quietly, and walks back to her desk. He sits back in his chair wearing a patient and attentive expression. She struggles, in vain, to pull her own chair from under her desk

and then shouts "Get Out!"
"But Miss, surely we should work this out; this could be a valuable opportunity for a Heated Debate..."

"Get out of my class!"

He can tell that she's only minutes away from tears now, on course to break all records. Her fists are pressed knuckles down on the desk, and there's a tremble in her arms.

"You know the way you were telling us about the Socratic tradition and all that..."

"This is your final warning, Jonathon. Out."

"Whoa, that's not a threat of physical violence, is it Miss? Because I might have to take that up with a higher authority..."

"I'm giving you a detention in three ... two ... one..."

He grabs his briefcase. "Miss, I can see you're feeling vulnerable right now, maybe it's That Time, whatever" he says, making for the door, "so I'm going to take a step back here and maybe we can take this up after the break. Take care now," and he closes the door behind him.

Miss Moriarty swallows deeply and sits down, trying to control her breathing, when the door snaps open and he pops his head back in.

"Just wanted to wish you a Merry Christmas, Miss."

8

"Dunk me, Mark!" shouts the Doc. "C'mon, slam it to me white-boy!" Of all the white-boys in the year, and they are all white, Mark could reasonably be accused of being the whitest. Also the tallest, the blondest, and the most vein-exposingly hairless.

It had been Mark's great misfortune, some time ago, to profess an enthusiasm for basketball during P.E. He couldn't shoot, he couldn't jump, he wasn't much of a passer, and when he dribbled up the court the ball would inevitably skitter off his impossible knees. But he was NBA tall and, despite lacking any real confidence, bolshy, which made him an irresistible target for the Doc's routines.

Mark is stuck outside the offensive D with the Doc buzzing around him at chest height, trash-talking and swiping at the ball in Mark's hands.

"C'mon peeps, take a shot, take a shot, put some air under it. Let it fly, peeps!"

Mark steps back on his unsteady right leg and patiently cups the ball in his enormous right hand, balancing with the left. Textbook shooting posture. He makes one very obvious feint, his whole body joining in the wasted effort, and releases the ball straight and true into the Doc's blocking hand.

"Rejection! Rejection, peeps!"

The Doc, indifferent to the fate of the ball, performs a quick victory dance to Mark's receding back. One of the Doc's team-mates gathers the ball at the sideline and passes it back into play.

The Doc on the ball now, thundering up the court, eyes glued to the ground, pounding the ball a foot further at a time, making slow but furious progress. Kieran Mulligan stolidly blocks his path. The Doc halts, takes aim at a spot between Mulligan's legs and slam-bounces it into his crotch. The ball softly rebounds back into the Doc's hands as Mr Scruton whistles to stop play.

"Foul and a turnover. Watch the dirty tactics, Feely."

"C'mon peeps, I was just trying to pass it between his legs! He got in the way!"

"Don't call me peeps, Mr Feely. Are you able to play on, Kieran?"

Mulligan, doubled over his mangled testes, holds up a finger to signal he'll be all right in a minute.

"Play ball!" shouts Scruton, on an indiscriminate American sports buzz.

Mark lopes back down to offence, the Doc marking him all the way, backing him off with the crouching ass manoeuvre that endeared him to basketball in the first place.

"I got you cold, peeps. You ain't goin' nowhere. Think you gonna dunk me, is that what you thinkin', peeps?"

"I never said I could dunk, Feely," says Mark in his deep, adenoidal voice, a voice too inflexible for humour, constrained between low and loud.

"Big tall glass of milky-white milk like you? Course you can dunk. But you ain't gonna dunk me, peeps. You the shit and I'm the fly, you the strawberries and I'm the cream; I'm all over you like Teflon, peeps."

The Doc doesn't know what Teflon is. He thinks it might be a kind of glue, but mostly he just likes the sound of it for trash-talking purposes.

"The fuck you talking about, Feely?"

"You gotta work on your comebacks, peeps, you just gotta."

Mark springs to catch a high ball. It ricochets off his clumsy fingers and the Doc pivots and snatches it. Mark lunges in gets a hold top and bottom.

"Think you can wrestle me, peeps? Think you got what it takes to wrestle with the alligator?"

"FUCK. OFF. FEELY."

"Language, Mark," says Scruton.

The Doc crooks his elbow round the ball and reefs from the shoulder, breaking Mark's hold. He begins his hard dribbling approach to the net, sufficiently slow and laboured for Mark to get the break on him and scoot out in front. The Doc fights him up to the D, at which point Mark slips in a puddle of sweat and falls, with the tragicomic buckling of the excessively tall and awkward. He collapses facing away from the Doc, who, without even blinking, takes a running leap up the ramp of Mark's back. He presses off between Marks shoulder blades, sails high, and flings the ball wildly in the vague direction of the net. The ball clears the backboard by a good twelve feet and Scruton's whistle is shrieking before his feet touch court again.

"Feely! Sin bin!"

"I was just catchin' air, peeps!"

"What did I say? What did I say?"

"I'm just jivin' here! I'm just jammin' with my good buddy, Mark!"

Mark is making heavy weather of getting off the ground.

"I've got a bad back you fucking shithead!"

"Just playin' a little hardball, peeps."

"Stop calling me 'peeps'! You're such a fucking asshole."

"Comebacks, peeps, you gotta work on your comebacks."

"Hit the showers, Mr Feely. And I want a five page essay on spinal injuries for Monday morning. And don't think I've forgotten term finishes today. I'll be here and so will you."

The Doc reverts to his normal voice.

"Ah, you're *taking* the *piss*!"

"Congratulations, now you've got detention too."

"Why are you all being such a bunch of bitches?"

"Two detentions. Keep going."

The Doc, sweat pouring off him like liquid rage, stands defiant. Twenty-five pairs of eyes watch him, waiting for another outburst. He can taste the stinging sweat salt on his lips and he can feel every single pair of eyes just willing him to make matters worse. Very softly, almost without moving his lips, he whispers in a voice strange to everyone, including himself – "Maybe I'll just stop taking the piss and chop your fucking heads off."

"What was that?" says Scruton.

The Doc is somewhat taken aback. He isn't sure he meant to say what he'd just said. Nor is he sure if he really said it at all.

"Nothing sir."

Scruton steps forward and gets up in his face.

"I asked you what you said."

The Doc glares at him, willing that smooth, blandly handsome face to explode. He *knows* he'd like that.

Scruton is actually quite sure of what he'd heard the Doc say, as are most of the students in the hall. He really just wants the Doc to have said something else, something he won't feel obliged to make a big fuss over on the last day of term.

The Doc holds Scruton's stare another moment and then – "What I said was… I'm sorry for taking the piss and I'll stop shooting my mouth off. Sir."

Scruton holds the Doc's gaze for another few seconds, to make sure the Doc knows he's treating this as a Very Serious Incident. Then he says, "Good. You do that. Showers."

The Doc stalks out of the hall and thumps into the dressing

rooms. Still fuming, he chops one off in the temporary privacy of the showers. His wank fantasy of Laura is polluted by thoughts of naked class-mates, which causes him a moment of sexual orientation queasiness, but he puts it down to the locker-room ambience. As he comes he imagines blood fountaining out of a headless torso.

9

Hulking, Neanderthalic Stephan Clarke perches on a high stool in the centre of the studio. Big of bone and sloping of brow, all that's needed to complete the primitive ambience is a gnawed animal leg, with partial pelt, to be nestling in his broad lap. This is an imaginative imposition Duke is attempting to excise from his mind before he puts pencil to paper.

Duke is aware, and has been aware for some time, that his renderings of real-life subjects tended to accentuate the grotesque and misshapen. And lately he's begun to wonder if this tendency might be significant of some more fundamental fault in his personality. If perhaps his portraits are expressive of a genuine cruel streak. And, furthermore, he wonders if he might not be above *relishing* this cruel streak.

A couple of weeks ago Ted McKenna had been the unwilling subject of the ten minute sketch. Ted was a wheezy, shifty rattle-bag of problems. Duke figured he probably had some very serious and undiagnosed social phobia. In five years, nine for those who had been in prep school with him, no one could remember having exchanged more than ten words with the guy. If Ted ever spoke out of turn (i.e. in any circumstance other than a mandatory class presentation) it was treated as a gossip worthy event. One afternoon the previous year, Ted had been sitting opposite Duke in the lunch hall and had taken the trouble to lean over his plate of chips and chicken wings to say to Duke, in his whispery, unmodulated tones: "Do you know what the time is?" Duke had felt specially chosen, had to fight the urge to gather witnesses and cry out, "Look! He speaks to me! Hearken to this unsolicited speech! Mark this wondrous day!" But he hadn't known what the time was, and he'd felt so guilty about not having the means to impart the hour that he'd asked his dad for a watch, just in case Ted ever reached out again. So far, he hadn't.

Ted, in addition to being extremely socially maladjusted, also had a slight hump-back. He'd developed (so Duke surmised) a strange, uneven walk to try to camouflage it, which really only made him look like he had a hump-back *and* one leg shorter than the other. In short, Ted was not an ideal candidate for the dispassionate scrutiny of a life-drawing class.

Nonetheless, Mr Kennedy, a dispassionate aesthete through and through, had one day plucked poor Ted from self-imposed obscurity and positioned him on the high stool. Duke hadn't thought about the sketch. In ten minutes there wasn't sufficient time for much in the way of conscious planning. He just drew what he saw, as (so he believed) did everyone else. But perhaps the other sketchers had been deliberately circumspect, mindful of the allowances one should make when drawing a subject so obviously sensitive about their appearance. Perhaps they had cruelty filters that Duke just lacked.

When time was called Mr Kennedy strolled between the easels examining the work. Harrumphs of displeasure and exclamations of praise would habitually erupt from Mr Kennedy on these inspection rounds. "Excellent!" "Rubbish!" "No grasp of the light!" "Supreme grasp of the light!" "Hideous! Absolutely hideous!" "Now!" he said, hoisting Duke's sketch so everyone could see, including Ted.

"This. Is. Exemplary! See how deftly the source light is conveyed! And the sweep of the hunched back! Perfectly captured!"

That was all there was to it – Mr Kennedy pointing out to all and sundry how perfectly Duke had rendered 'the sweep of the hunched back!'. He was speaking literally of course. Dispassionate aesthetic contemplation has no time for people's 'feelings'. But where Mr Kennedy saw only a clear-sighted and technically adept representation of a given object, the communal feeling was that Duke had created something macabre, something disturbingly *intimate*; as though he'd snuck into Ted's private House of Horrors and lifted his image straight from the warped looking-glass of his imagination. And that Ted's physical deformity should be so publicly acknowledged, and by a *teacher*, by a card-carrying adult member of the Real World ... it was just too much to bear.

Duke had studiously avoided looking at Ted to gauge his reaction, as, he imagined, did everyone else. Ted's feelings on the matter, like Ted's feelings on every matter, went unrecorded. But it was a safe bet that this wasn't going to lead to a major break-through for the guy.

After the fact, 'Duke's Elephant Man' was the subject of much anecdotal analysis. The Doc maintained that Duke had, coldly, and with malice afore thought, orchestrated the entire affair. "You love that sick shit, dontcha?" he'd said, genuinely impressed at such a novel method of bullying. "I mean, you knew, you just *knew* Kennedy would show it off and say something like that, didn't you?"

Duke hadn't known, and he hadn't intended on pioneering a new brand of psychological terrorism. But he hadn't denied it outright either. For one thing, strenuous denials were tiresome. For another, the notion of Duke picking on Ted was contemptible and, frankly, he'd expect people to know that if he were to consciously bring out the big guns he'd choose a worthier quarry ... but in the end, the reason he didn't set the Doc straight was that he found his accusations flattering. It was gratifying to the ego to be considered such a mastermind of deviancy. And sophisticated piss-taking, as in nearly any male environment, was like currency in Xavier – you just put it in your piggy bank and let your reputation grow.

His current sketch of Clarky isn't any good. He's been cautious about letting the personal enter into his composition and the portrait has suffered as a result.

Bland, he decides.

In art, at least, it was probably better to be of the Doc's party.

Bob comes up to him at the end of class and says, "Here, check this out."

He rests a jotter on Duke's easel and opens it to a page headlined 'Exponential Offensiveness Gradiant of the Doc's Boating Shoes'. Beneath are three drawings of Dubarry shoes in profile. Bob adopts a mock-professorial style and wields his ruler like a baton. "As we can see in figure one the standard 'boating shoe' becomes offensive at two points; one, in the space between the cuff of the trouser leg and the aperture of the shoe."

The ruler indicates the aforementioned space on the diagram marked 'Fig.1'.

"Maximal indecency is reached when the space between cuff and shoe exceeds two inches and the subject is combining, against every rule of style and decency, white socks with a black 'boating shoe'."

The ruler indicates a line just beneath the cuff, entitled, in red ink, 'Line of Indecency'.

"In figure two we can see how the standard boating shoe becomes objectionable here."

Bob draws a curved line through the toe of the 'standard boating shoe'.

"However, the Doc's boating shoe, being of a clownish length, extends far past this point."

'Fig.3' shows the Doc's exceptionally long boating shoe.

"The Doc's shoe is also curved like a banana, which as we

know is the most phallic of fruits, which increases the fuck-off factor by about five million percent. When all these factors are combined we arrive at what I like to call the Event Horizon of Offensiveness, which is a sort of black hole from which no decency can escape."

He turns the page to reveal 'Fig.4'. It is a picture of a man wearing a shirt and tie (and squared-off glasses) and nothing else. His tiny, hairy button of a penis peeps out from between the folds of the shirt.

"I just can't decide what's worse; if he's got a boner or if he's flaccid."

"I think, in this case, small is best," says Duke. "And I think it's missing one little detail."

"Be my guest."

Duke takes out a marker and draws a neat red circle underneath the glasses on the stickman's face. The trouserless businessman immediately becomes an off-duty clown. Bob nods at the page and passes his final judgment.

10

After he leaves the locker rooms, Doc decides to skip math class. He doesn't make skipping class into an elaborate performance; he just walks out of the sports centre, goes past the art rooms, cuts by the entrance to the science block and ambles calmly along the corridor within view of the staff-rooms. He even meets the headmaster emerging from the staff toilets, trailing a slipstream of powerful cologne. They nod to each other like mutually respectful professionals and go their separate ways. Escaping is so easy he wonders why he doesn't do this every day. He pokes his head into the canteen and sees that the side door is open. The door is open because Wayne, the angry young head chef of the canteen, is having a sneaky cigarette.

"Bum a smoke, Wayne?" says the Doc.

Wayne frowns at him and says, "You cutting class, Doc?"

"Taking a long lunch."

"Why not," says Wayne, and he hands over a cigarette.

Then he's out in the grounds. He walks by the old tennis courts and into the murky green of the tree-lined avenue that leads to the back gate. The gate is locked but it's easy to get over the fence from this side by shinning up an ivy-wrapped tree and swinging from a bough into the street. Once out on the street and beyond the eyes of teachers, he lights his cigarette with the Clipper he always keeps handy and then goes looking for a good spot to lie in wait for Dukey.

When the bell rings to signal the end of Art class and the start of the lunch break, Duke gathers his things and heads out the front door of the school. He skirts round the edge of the lawn and walks down the drive. The journey to his house is longer going by the drive and up the Sandford Road rather than out the back gate but he invents a desire for a Coffee Society muffin in order to justify the detour. There is a real reason for the detour but he decides not to think about that because it might make him feel guilty.

The Doc settles for the church. The church and the grounds offer many good lurking places, and of a high gothic pedigree too. The church also looms at the apex of the two streets that lead to Beechwood Avenue, where Duke lives, so he'll have to walk down at least one of them to get home for lunch. The Doc walks around the church, reading the Latin inscriptions carved into the granite, inscriptions that he doesn't understand but likes the sound of. He makes haw ghosts with his breath, and blows them around a stone cross. A dizzy spell clouds his eyes and loosens his knees for a few seconds, and he realises that it's at least sixteen hours since he ate anything. He hopes Duke has some good food at the house.

Duke knows the Doc is currently on some residential back street in Ranelagh, crouched behind a bush or a parked car, or standing flat against a wall and pretending to be a spy or a fugitive or a leprous derelict or a psychopathic businessman, and waiting for Duke to pass by so he can stalk him for a bit, maybe terrorise him with some weird noises, and then slip silently into step beside him. Duke's part in the game is simple: he allows himself to be stalked and when the Doc decides the stalking game is played out, Duke's job is to pick up the thread of some conversation or routine from days or months past. Then Duke will let them into the house and the Doc will tear through the kitchen, pawing the food Duke's mum had laid out that morning.

He mulls over the problem of how to distance oneself from a friend. What do you say? I think we've been spending too much time together? Maybe we could do with a break? I'd like to start seeing other people? The answer, he knows, is that you don't say anything, unless you want to actively invite the charge of major gayness. Instead you take a different route home and invent excuses for missing phone calls. And then, afterwards, you say, "We just sort of grew apart."

At the door of Coffee Society he falters for a second when he sees a very pissed-off looking Houghton and a very hung over looking Chris sitting with Laura and a circle of aggressively chatty Muckross girls, all in their uniforms of green polyester, platinum blond hair and orange skin. He notices that Laura, even though it's a school day, is wearing more make-up than she was wearing last night, and can't help but give her a few demerit points for such base tribal conformity. He mumbles a non-committal "hey" to Houghton and Laura as he passes on the way to the coffee dock and then makes a tit of himself by ordering "just a black coffee" in a voice loud enough to be overheard. By now the alibi of a chocolate muffin has transformed into a genuine desire for a chocolate muffin but something reflexive makes him order the coffee instead.

And why would I do that? he wonders. Is it because she'll suddenly drop her boyfriend when she perceives my hard-bitten masculinity as reflected by my choice of cafe purchase? Is it because if I choose something sweet and chocolatey and therefore unmanly I may ruin my chances forever? Is that why? You idiot, Dukey.

He moves to the end of the bar to wait for his coffee and catches Houghton's eye to try to figure out whether or not he's the subject of any suspicions. Houghton looks back and nods, but only as a gesture of masculine solidarity. His patience is clearly being tested by the company. Chris is staring into the middle distance like he wants to punch it. Laura avoids eye contact altogether. She is wearing a pair of fingerless pink gloves, from which he deduces that the cigarette burning hasn't yet become public knowledge. Relieved, Duke tunes in to the conversation, which is primarily conducted by two lividly fake tanned girls with identical voices, both very hoarse (*though they'd probably prefer the word 'husky'*, thinks Duke) and pitching their words at a volume implying utter disregard for the fact that everyone in the café can hear them. Their voices are so similar it's almost a monologue.

"I was like, Oh you definitely would, and then I hear he's wearing fake tan and I'm like, Have I got great taste? And for fuck's sake, like, seriously, a guy shaving his legs? Please."

"Well, like, if a girl didn't make the effort a guy would be like, 'You should make the effort'. You know, like? So guys should make an effort too, like."

"Yeah, but, like, when a guy starts shaving his legs and wearing fake tan it's just, like, crossing a line."

"Yeah, but, like, if he takes care of his hair and his clothes, that's fine, like, and years ago, you know like, back in the day, guys didn't do that, so now it's different, like."

"Okay, but, like, Roddy was saying about how, like, he was going into BT2 to buy Jean Paul Gaultier foundation with Doug which is just, like... Guys are just girls now, like. It's not just metrosexual, they're just becoming, like, total bitches."

On 'bitches' Houghton and Duke look at each other with disbelieving eyes, struggle to hold it together for a second, and then burst out laughing simultaneously. Duke intercepts the barista who is putting his coffee on the bar and waves a hand to apologise for being incapacitated with the giggles. He presses a plastic lid round the rim and, still laughing, walks out the door.

The church is close enough to the school, and the air sufficiently still for the sound of the lunch bell to carry to the Doc. Because he's been waiting for half an hour already he fully expects Duke to arrive seconds after the three peals ring out. When he doesn't the Doc feels instantly stood up. Five minutes later, after being passed by other Xavier boys going home for lunch, he wonders if he somehow hasn't noticed Duke walking by or if he really has been stood up.

He abandons the church and walks down to Duke's house on Mornington Road. Through the downstairs window he can see some bread and fruit and jars on the kitchen table, all untouched, but he rings the doorbell anyway. On the fifth unanswered ring he slams the knocker hard enough to loose a crackling shower of paint flecks onto the stoop. Then he turns heel and storms down to the main road.

His mood turns thunderous when he walks by Coffee Society and sees Duke standing over Houghton and Laura and a crowd of Muckross girls. He doubles back from the plate glass window before they spot him and crosses the road to a bus-stop where he can observe from a safe distance. He sits on a step beside a petite woman of indeterminable age who is gripping the handles of a buggy with unmistakeably maternal vigilance. In the buggy is the biggest baby the Doc has ever seen; a vast, air clutching sea slug of a child. He looks from the waiflike mother to her monstrous child, marvelling at the woman's tiny waist, her pencil thin legs, and hips that he could put his hands around with fingers and thumbs touching.

He turns back to the café and sees Duke and Houghton laughing. Duke is laughing so hard he has to bend forward and balances his heaving weight on his knees. Houghton's big square head is thrown all the way back so, in the silent profile presented to the Doc, he looks like he's screaming at something on the ceiling.

What the fuck? wonders the Doc. *The funniest joke ever told?*

The Doc's sudden worry is that Houghton has actually managed to say or do something incredibly funny. For a second he even has a vision of Duke carrying on a wise-cracking friendship on the side, not just on the side but behind the Doc's back, and with Houghton too; clearly one of the least funny people in the whole school. If Houghton can be funny then the world will never make sense again.

Duke comes out of the café. He's still so caught up with whatever comedy spectacular has just transpired that he doesn't see the Doc standing directly opposite him on the far side of the road. Then he heads towards Mornington.

The Doc takes a deep breath and stands. Before leaving he rounds on the woman and her baby. He fixes her with his livid gaze and points a finger at her colossal child. Her eyes widen in genuine panic.

"I was just wondering," he says, in the tone of a man who doesn't like being lied to but expects nothing better of the world. "Did that really come out of you?"

She blinks and opens her mouth wordlessly, as though trying to come up with a defence or a put-down, but the Doc doesn't care about right of reply. He turns away from her, runs across the road and follows Duke home.

11

At the front door of his house, Duke pats his pockets for the key and then remembers it's in his school bag. He leans down to put his coffee on the stoop so he can swing his bag off his back and suffers a moment of brain-freezing panic when he sees the Doc smiling at him from the neighbours' side of the dividing hedge.

"Dooo-key."

The Doc's Cheshire Cat smile, wide and white, effloresces from the briary darkness. Duke snort-laughs through his nose, and wonders if he looks guilty.

"What you up to, Dookey?" says the Doc, coyly, as though he were about to ask if Duke already had a date for the prom.

"Just. Going in for some food."

"Sounds scrumptious."

Duke stands up and the Doc walks round to his side of the hedge. They stand there for a second as Duke tries to wait him out. Duke figures that just once, just once in the entire history of their friendship, it would be nice to receive an actual request, a 'do you mind' or 'is it okay if I join' – but the Doc is still wearing his 'coy request' face and it's too stomach-churning to bear.

"Would you like to come in, Doc," he says, with a touch of what he hopes is weary condescension, hoping to perhaps extort a note of courtesy or gratitude.

"Sure," says the Doc, "no problem good buddy, I'll keep you company. We don't want you chowing down all by your lonesome, now do we?"

Duke puts his bag on the ground and looks for his key. He sees the envelope and says, "I got your letter."

"What letter?"

"The letter. With the meat? At least I think it was meat."

"Meat? In a letter? What sick fuck would put meat in a letter? Was it by any chance a nice juicy chop?"

"It was a fuckin' mouldy piece of jerky. It looked like the bowel movement of Tutankhamen."

"So did you eat it? Did you make a delicious sandwich? Smothered in mayo and barbeque sauce between thick slices of rye bread, washed down with a fruity Beaujolais?"

"Yes, that's what I did..."

"You're such a sick fuck, Dookey."

Having failed to find his key Duke upends the entire contents of his bag onto the pavement and starts flicking through his books. "You know I'm pretty sure it's illegal to send meat in the post. That thing was a biological hazard. It was practically an act of terrorism. I hope you get locked up and raped. I hope they abuse you the way you abuse Doogie."

"How dare you! This is fucking outrageous! I love Doogie, and Doogie loves his master. Sometimes Doogie just requires discipline. Spare the rod and spoil the dog..."

"Doogie is severely disturbed, Doc," says Duke in his blandest tones. "I've been to your house. I've seen the poor, traumatised little beastie quivering in his corner whenever anyone comes through the door. He's a basket-case."

"He only shakes like that because he's happy to see his beloved master..."

"No, he shakes like that because he palsied with mortal terror. And you know the way he obsessively licks that patch on the kitchen wall? That's not normal canine behaviour."

"He thinks it's a tasty treat!"

"Face it Doc, Doogie's an obsessive-compulsive, agoraphobic, moulting, *incontinent* nut-job. The most loving act would be to shoot him in the head..."

"No! Doogie!"

"...and put him out of his misery. Your dad seems like the type to have a gun in the house. I'd even volunteer my mercy-killing services..."

"You have no comprehension of the sacred bond between a man and his Doogie. Sometimes I have to wonder about you. I really do."

"Well, sometimes I have to wonder about you, Doc."

"Meaning?"

"Well, for starters, *I* haven't tried to kill anyone today..."

"What d'you mean?"

Duke realises that there's a spare under the mat. He gathers up his books and shoves them back in his bag.

"Seriously, what are you talking about?" says the Doc.

"Nothing. Forget it."

Duke flips the mat over to reveal the cling wrapped key and, even as he does so, chides himself for letting the Doc see.

"No, seriously," says the Doc.

"Do you *really* not know?" says Duke, unwrapping the slimy cling film. "Are you utterly mystified?"

"No. I mean yeah, what the fuck are you talking about?"

"You're actually going to make me spell it out, aren't you? You're..."

Duke sighs at the Doc's blanket refusal to play the game of honest conversation.

"Benno?" says Duke. "Today? You wielding a tree trunk like a chimp trying to break a nut? A look of homicidal glee in your eyes? Is any of this familiar?"

"So what? I didn't do anything, did I? It was just... boisterous play."

"Anyway," he continues, "he slapped me in the face. He was begging for some discipline."

"I'm pretty sure you slapped him first..." says Duke.

"Look, we could spend all day arguing about who slapped who first, and how hard..."

"It was you!"

"It's a moat point."

"You mean *moot*. 'It's a moot point'. And it isn't. But forget it."

He lets them in. On the left, off the short corridor, is the kitchen, which the Doc makes for with unseemly haste. As always in Duke's corner of artisan Arcadia, his mother has left out fruit and cheeses (so they'd be at room temperature when he got in) and a freshly baked ciabatta. The Doc falls to slicing and sampling immediately.

"Oh, don't mind me, just help yourself," says Duke, standing clear of the massacre of his food.

"Yeah thanks. Haven't eaten all day," says the Doc, turning his attention to the fridge. "Do you have any juicy chops?"

"No. There's some baby squid in brine."

"No shit?"

"Check the back."

The Doc snouts into the fridge and rummages destructively. Duke hears an 'uugh' of disgust and then the Doc extracts a glass jar packed tight with multi-legged, bulbous headed creatures. The Doc, an unrepentant culinary philistine, turns the jar over in his hands, examining the contents carefully. Finally, in a voice heavy with incredulity, he says "Do you eat these?"

"Daily."

"Bullshit. You can't, you're a vegan."

"I'm a vegetarian. And if you ever paid any attention in biology you'd know that squid are closely related to marine plant life."
"Absolute bullshit."

"It's true. They evolved from sea anemones, which are the marine link between plant-life and animal life. Ergo, you know, QED. Why do you think squid are called 'flowers of the sea'?"

"You're talking out of your ass," says the Doc, but his resolve is weakening against this scientific and etymological 'evidence'.

Duke shrugs, curious to see how far he can push it.

"I'm just quoting Darwin on this. I don't find squid any less disgusting because they're basically just mobile plants. Frankly, I wish I had an excuse not to eat them. But they're a good source of vegetarian protein."

Duke wonders how many fantastical facts he's managed to squeeze into the Doc's reason-resistant head. If the Doc fulfilled some of his Travis Bickle style tendencies they might one day be regurgitated to the world, indexed into an ever expanding taxi-drivers encyclopaedia of spurious claims and trenchant nonsense. Duke's legacy to the world.

"Ok," says the Doc, "eat it."

Duke has already steeled himself for the ace card. There was, to be fair, a masochistic thrill to the challenge.

"Sure. I was going to have one anyway."

The Doc unscrews the lid of the jar. He jabs unsuccessfully at the slippery aliens with a fork, loses himself in the fascination of testing squid buoyancy, eventually remembers what he's supposed to be doing, and lays down the fork in favour of a tablespoon. He scoops one into the bowl of the spoon and it sits there, trembling in a puddle of brine, its tentacles just overlapping the metal circumference.

"Just imagine that it's a nice juicy chop," says the Doc.

It still has eyes, not even eyes; pinprick black light-receptors. And somewhere in the centre of that slimy flower of tentacles is a minuscule beak, which would have chomped its way through the shells of delicate crabs. The skin is grey and smooth and rubbery and the mention of juicy chops sets off tingles in Duke's mouth and stomach, sensory memories of supple, fibrous textures. This would be the first flesh to pass his lips in over two years. And the first squid full stop.

The Doc aeroplanes the spoon at his face.

"Open wii-ide."

Duke snatches the squid off the spoon before the Doc can

shove it into his mouth. The Doc tries to force the salty spoon between Duke's lips regardless, his expression fraught with concentration, like an intrepid pearl-diver attempting to jemmy an oyster. Duke pokes a finger into his cheek and the Doc darts away. He hates anyone touching his face.

"I'm *trying* to eat my squid," says Duke, trying to imagine that the squid is an artichoke.

Duke opens his mouth as wide as he can and places the head of the squid on the lip of his lower incisors, bites down and yanks at the tentacled torso. Something like a grisly plug connected to the tentacles pops out of a socket in the head. The mechanism is as neat as a Kinder Surprise toy. He wills his jaw muscles to contract and bite down on the gobstopper.

Do squids have brains? Or just a ganglion of nerves? Is one less disgusting than the other?

He compresses the disembodied head between his molars and it shoots over to the other side of his mouth. His stomach prepares to climb up his throat and run away.

"Toughie, is it?" says the Doc.

Duke starts chewing savagely, knowing he's lost this round. Unidentifiable liquids burst from the cranium and coat his mouth. He swallows the ragged flesh whole, choking it down the gullet. Eventually he gets it all in there. He keeps very still. The slightest tremor might bring it back up. He makes satisfied noises.

"Mmm. Delicious."

"Now the rest," says the Doc, with the blank manner of a pure sadist.

"No. No, you just eat the head."

"But the legs are the best bit, right? Isn't that what camalari's made of?"

"Calamari. Not this species, though," says Duke, "they have, ehh, ink-sacs in the leg-torso section."

He chucks the remaining squid matter in the bin before the Doc can force the issue and stifles a retch.

The Doc, for his part, sits at the kitchen table happily munching through a huge sandwich of cheese and condiments between four-fifths of the ciabatta. He's made an infuriating concession to etiquette by leaving the crusty end piece for Duke.

"You know what your problem is, Dookey," says the Doc, spraying masticated bits of sandwich over the table. "You lack a sense of irony."

Duke can sense from the reflective and 'ethical' note in the

Doc's voice that he is referring back to the earlier conversation about Benno. Duke wonders how long he'd been waiting to use the smart sounding phrase.

"Is that right?"

"Yep," says the Doc, leaning back and crossing his legs for a properly sententious pose. "No sense of irony at all sometimes."

"And what exactly do you mean by 'irony', Doc?"

Duke has no problem playing the sententious game.

"You know. Irony."

"Repeating it doesn't explain it."

"It's like ... you know what I mean ... like. Irony. Sense of humour about certain situations."

"Nope, not following you."

"Well, you're so fuckin' smart you explain it," says the Doc, caught short and bristling.

"You're actually pretty good at irony, Doc. You often say one thing and mean the opposite. Or, at the very least, you mean something else."

"Yeah, but that's like, sarcasm," says the Doc witheringly, "I mean explain it like a definition."

"Okay, a definition," says Duke, mulling for a second. "Okay. Alright. There's this guy, right..."

"A businessman?"

"Yeah. Sure, a businessman. And he has to go to a meeting. In New York. He works in Boston and he has to go to New York for the meeting. And the meeting is that afternoon. So he should really get on a short-hop flight. But this businessman is terrified of flying. So he gets in his car and speeds off to New York and he makes the meeting just in time..."

"What's the meeting for?"

"It doesn't matter what the meeting's for!"

"But what line of business is he in? It's all in the details, Dookey."

"Okay, fine, he's a, he's a lawyer and he's meeting with the State Department to talk about an amnesty on Arabs interned in Guantanamo Bay..."

"He's defending towel-heads?"

"Precisely. Shut up a second. So, anyway, they're all tucking into their Danishes or whatever and then a newsflash comes on about a plane flying from Boston to New York – this is the plane he was supposed to get on, right – a plane that's been hijacked by escapees from Guantanamo Bay. And just as the business man..."

"Lawyer."

"Just as the *lawyer* is thanking his lucky stars that he chose not to fly today the plane smashes through the window and kills him. *How Ironic.* An unsentimental observer might remark. And so many levels, if I say so myself. There you go."

The Doc slowly digests the story.

"It's a bit long for a definition, isn't it?"

"Well it's more of an anecdotal example."

"Have you got anything shorter?"

"Well, you know, there are different kinds of irony; dramatic irony, Socratic irony, Tarantino irony, though I don't know if he qualifies any more…"

"Definition. *De-fi-ni-tion.*"

"Irony is like. The joke that you don't get. Until it's too late."

"The Joke. That you don't get. Until it's too late," repeats the Doc, a mocking pastiche of philosophical meditation.

"Yeah," he says. "Do you have any biscuits?"

12

Duke chooses a good viewing seat for Irish class. The Doc, loaded up on sandwich and chocolate digestives, has been on a gibbering sugar high all the way back from the house. It bodes well for another entertaining episode of Irish Four, also known as Cabbage Irish, last refuge of the linguistically challenged.

Red-eyed Mr Macken presides, by turns exasperated and amused at the ineptitude of his charges. They are; Duke, the Doc, Julian (sitting as far from the blackboard as possible, muttering over a Latin textbook as though to raise the spirits of Cicero and Catullus), the Boss (absent, still at Bob's place), Beckerman (pretending to sleep), Bob (placidly stoned), Diego (son of the Brazilian ambassador, only obliged to sit in with Irish Four because the library is being renovated) and Mark (the sole class member who holds out hope for a promotion from the quagmire of Irish Four, to the lofty academic promontory of Irish Three, where he might at least stop forgetting the words he already knows).

After just two weeks in charge of his crew of linguistic incompetents, Mr Macken had effectively resigned his sacred duty to impart the mysteries of the native tongue. He still made the occasional stab at bona fide course work, but by now, four months into term, the students had thoroughly filleted the class in order to yield maximum diversion. Videos, crosswords and hangman had swiftly edged out the curriculum. Duke was sure a colouring-in module couldn't be far behind; a Kindergarten atmosphere was prevailing at such an alarming rate that soon they'd be arguing over who got the good crayons and stopping class due to little 'accidents'.

The Doc had spear-headed this infantilising movement. He'd sold Mr Macken on the notion of devoting Friday's class to what he called 'Storytime'. The original deal had been for short, performative compositions delivered in Irish and subsequently added to and improved by the class. The Doc, however, had shanghaied 'Storytime' into an open-mic forum for whatever demented rubbish happened to be clogging his channels.

He makes the request to begin as soon as Mr Macken gets to his desk. "It's that time sir."

"No, Jonathon. I'm revoking 'Storytime' privileges this week."

"Sir! We had an agreement!"

"The agreement only covered stories written and performed as Gaeilge. So far, to the best of my recollection, none of your stories have been as Gaeilge. I assume you have a story for today's class, yes?"

"I was up all night, sir. It may be my superwork."

Masterpiece, thinks Duke. *Genius.*

"And have you composed this latest opus as Gaeilge?"

"Not entirely sir. I thought it might be an enjoyable translation exercise for the class."

"No doubt, Jonathon, but your stories so far have proved somewhat resistant to translation..."

"That just means it'll be an exciting challenge for a scholar like yourself, sir."

Julian pipes up and all eyes fall on him. His voice quivers with agitation.

"Sir! Do we have to listen to him? Seriously, is it not a complete waste of class time? His fucking stories aren't even funny!"

Everyone shudders at Julian's outburst, which is, characteristically, far too vociferous to be taken seriously. Mr Macken rolls his eyes and emits a teacherly clucking sound, yielding the floor. Experience has taught him that there's little to be gained by going head to head with the Doc.

"Okay," says the Doc, clicking open his briefcase and taking out a foolscap pad. He stands for extra effect, holds the pad before him and flicks past doodles and scribbles and old death lists to the designated page. As Mr Macken sits directly in front of the Doc he is unable to see what Duke, being a row behind and to the left, can see; that the page the Doc is about to 'read' from is completely blank. "Okay," says the Doc again. "It's called 'Varsity Zombies', sir."

"Just ... get on with it, Jonathon," says Mr Macken, rolling his eyes and inhaling like someone preparing to undergo extreme pain, though everyone knows this is mostly an act; Mr Macken is one of the few teachers who seems to get the Doc's humour.

"It's really more of a movie script."

The Doc's eyes scorch the blank page. He begins.

"Interior of a typical American High School. A corridor with tall metal lockers either side."

"Dorchla le taisceadain arda miotail ar an da thaobh."

"Eh, yeah."

The Doc concentrates fiercely for a few seconds, his eyes

screwed up, his mouth working through a few potential openers.

Then it's like something ... just ... lifts. And he's off.

"'James Van Der Beek is strutting confidently down the corridor, wearing an American football jersey, a football helmet and jock-strap. He tosses and catches a pigskin. We see - a nerd, played by Skeet Ulrich, standing beside a locker, wiping down the plastic dust-cover on a comic-book."

"Caitheann se ding gruaige i lar a chloiginn, oh just go ahead..."

"Yeah, sure, thanks sir. Uhh – Van Der Beek throws the pigskin with star-quarterback accuracy and dinks Skeet Ulrich on the side of the head, knocking off his glasses. Skeet Ulrich: 'Leave me alone, Van Der Beek. *You used to be a geek too, Dawson*'. Van Der Beek: 'Eat pigskin, Nerdlinger. You're the poor man's Johnny Depp.' Van Der Beek makes Skeet Ulrich EAT the PIGSKIN. Skeet Ulrich writhes LIKE A MAGGOT in Van Der Beek's STRONG MANLY HOLD."

The Doc's voice becomes louder and more frenzied. "Suddenly Orlando Bloom bursts out of a locker. He staggers towards Van Der Beek and Skeet Ulrich with his arms outstretched. Orlando Bloom: 'Brains. Brains.' Van Der Beek: 'Hey, Orlando, what's going down? You wanna beat up on Skeet Ulrich with me?' Orlando Bloom: 'Brains.'"

The Doc rips out the page and scrumples it as he talks. "Skeet Ulrich: 'Oh my jiminy-jillickers! Orlando Bloom has been a zombie the whole time!' Van Der Beek: 'I just thought he was just a really bad actor!' Orlando Bloom sinks his PEARLY WHITES into Van Der Beek's MEATY THIGH. Van Der Beek's eyes glaze over. An ERECT ZOMBIE PENIS BURSTS from his jock-strap."

"Jonathon!" shouts Mr Macken.

The Doc throws the balled-up paper and it ricochets off Julian's head. "Van Der Beek begins to vigorously SODOMISE Skeet Ulrich."

"Jonathon, would you stop – Jonathon, stop humping your desk!" says Mr Macken helplessly, and the class dissolve into giggles. "Zombie Orlando Bloom gnaws at Van Der Beek's football helmet. His Hollywood teeth splinter and shards fall from his mouth. CHRISTIAN SLATER SPRINTS down the corridor. He has a whistle tied around his neck. He is the coach. Christian Slater: 'No fuckin' way! My star-fuckin' quarterback! Die, you cocksuckin' zombie Orlando Bloom!' Christian Slater tears Zombie Orlando Bloom off Van Der Beek and PUMMELS him. BUT the sight of his star quarterback's EXPOSED BUTTOCKS and Zombie Orlando Bloom's TOOTHLESS GUMS AROUSES him. He WHIPS OUT his stubby ROCKET COCK. Christian Slater: 'I've always wanted to try this.'"

"STOP!"

Mr Macken stands at his desk, hands clenched, visibly shaking with apoplexy.

"Jonathon…" he says.

"Sir?" The Doc stares back at him, both hands gripping the pad.

"You're bleeding," says Mr Macken.

"Whe… " the Doc begins to say. His tongue snakes out and explores the surrounding area, and retreats back into his mouth coated with in warm, thick blood.

"Oh…"

He takes out his rotten hanky, which still reeks of ether, and holds it to his nose.

"Maybe you should go to the bathroom and clean yourself up," says Mr Macken.

13

The Doc steps into the corridor and pulls the classroom door behind him. He stands still for a moment, takes the hanky away from his nose and sniffs. The blood flow seems to have dried up. He waits for his burning cheeks to cool, and wills them back to their usual pallor while listening to his breathing. His breath is so loud and distinct it's like an audio track inside his head. He starts walking down the corridor, indulging his light-headedness by pretending he's just been in a fight.

Motherfucker cracked you square in the snout there, Pat.

He lilts and sways on stupefied legs, adding drunkenness to the fantasy. He imagines a camera lingering in tender close-up on his blood stained profile. The shot tracks backwards to take in his shambling gait.

His shambling but dignified gait, he corrects himself.

Jump-cut to; Int. Toilet Cubicle. The Doc is on the bowl, his face washed clean. His trousers and boxers are around his ankles, and he beats off with a discreet minimum of noise and vibration. Suddenly, and without recorded precedent, he stays his trusty right hand. The camera holds its gaze at a respectful close-up, head and shoulders only. From the frozen-mid-motion set of the shoulders and the slight deepening of the brow we can deduce that A Plan Is Forming.

Cut to; a determined, striding Doc, straight-lining it to the next class, taking corners with exaggerated sharpness, forcing others to weave around him.

We See; the lanky fourth year, recipient of the chest-kicking earlier, walking the opposite way and spying an opportunity for a little get-back.

The Doc, in all honesty, doesn't even recognise this insignificant foe but some brute and canny instinct does recognise the trajectory of the walk and the intent to bang shoulders. Automatic defence mechanisms slide into place. At the last second our smooth operator side-steps to the left and gives his briefcase an extra-special swing, discreetly but precisely into the fourth years kneecap, and continues on his way. He restrains himself from looking back.

Damn, thinks the Doc. *Pat cuts through the low-lifes like they aren't even there.*

The Doc gets to class early, goes to the very back of the room and slides his briefcase under the last desk on the left. In order to be out of the way of anyone's peripheral vision he swiftly pulls every desk in the back row, apart from his own, a couple of feet forward. He takes the added precaution of removing the two seats nearest him and stacking them by the blackboard. All is in readiness when Ms Fasquelle glides through the door.

No student of Xavier addresses Ms Rene Fasquelle as Ms Fasquelle. They address her as 'Ms Rene'; an arrangement that suits all parties, appealing to Ms Rene's incorrigible coquetry and the boys' drooling appreciation of said incorrigible coquetry.

Ms Rene is young, French and delectable. Ms Rene has a Gioconda smile, quick brown eyes and a perfect body. Ms Rene is a dream. And, like a dream, Ms Rene cannot be touched. But how they *yearn.* Since arriving at Xavier at the start of term and taking over Continental languages, Ms Rene has achieved almost total dominance in the sexual daydream market, and made tremendous strides in the night time sector too. And, to top it off, Ms Rene is kind. Ms Rene is even kind to the Doc. Ms Rene never persecutes him or his clunking French, and he adores her for it.

This is the Doc's usual Friday routine: usually, after lunch, the Doc hijacks Irish class with a readymade routine, a snappy little cut-up from his favourite T.V. shows, movies or video-games, much like today. Pacified by the cathartic effects of performance the Doc usually toddles into Ms Rene's class and sleepily submits to a dose of double French. With woozy eyes he studies and records Ms Rene's posture and proportions, how she bends and straightens herself, the crafty interaction of fabric and flesh, and taking all these particulars he edits together a little internal home-video. Usually speaking. And, usually speaking, these feminine particulars would be drawn on later in the day, in the privacy of his bedroom, for a post-prandial bout of loving self-abuse.

But today is not a usual day. Something is happening to the Doc. He doesn't know if things are falling apart or if they're coming together. He doesn't know if he's breaking away or breaking through. He really doesn't know. He's just going with it.

Ms Rene is perched on her desk, her pretty head thrust forward from girlishly hunched shoulders, giving her boys some time to settle down and ready themselves for the lesson. Outside the sun is very low over the pitches. The light cuts through the tree line and bathes Ms Rene in golden lustre. Does she know the effect she has on her boys by perching at the front of her desk, her pencil skirts riding high on sculpted thighs? *Of course I know*, Ms Rene would say if she were ever quizzed in confidence about her pedagogical methods. *We all have our ways of holding their attention, mais non?*

Of course she knows, the Doc would say. *She's a beautiful woman. She's a cocktease. She loves it.*

Ms Rene speaks. Her voice burbles with Continental promise. "We are going to revise the soob-jonc-teef for a few minutes - just a few minutes, don't look so unhappy - and then, because it is the last day of term I thought it would be nice to watch a movie."

Exclamations of praise and relief from the class. The Doc takes off his jumper and lays it in his lap. He leans forward over the preset foolscap pad and crooks the shield of his right arm protectively around it, the pen in his hand poised in the ready-to-write-position.

I am a diligent student. I am eager to learn.

"Is that okay with everyone?" she says, smiling munificently, already confident of their goodwill. The Doc's left hand (for he is ambidextrous in this regard) scuttles beneath the desk and squats warmly in the crutch of his trousers.

"Bon. Michel..."

While Michel works through a conjugation the Doc wills his cock erect. He can tell it's going to be a slow-burner. Sometimes the best wanks come to those who wait.

Ms Rene listens to her beloved language fall flat and heavy from the Irish mouths, and smiles encouragingly through it all. The Doc, a little more in love with every tender word and gesture, starts rubbing the base of the shaft, kneading and compressing through the fabric of his trousers. His eyes scan up and down her legs, noting the shift of her flesh as she changes weight from one buttock to the other. Her black skirt rides just over her knees.

After ten minutes Ms Rene calls a halt to grammar. She pulls out the dolly mounted AV unit from its home in the corner. One helpful boy turns off the overhead fluorescent lights and another draws the Venetian blinds.

Much bending and prodding from Ms Rene as she interprets the mysteries of the DVD/TV interface.

The Doc moves his hand inside his pants.

After a long but victorious ordeal with technology Ms Rene

withdraws to the side and leans against the radiator beneath the windows. The line of seated students in front of the Doc have all moved their desks away from the windows to get a better angle on the monitor, presenting Ms Rene in profile to the Doc's all consuming eye. It is a testament to the ferocity of his concentration that the flickering screen fails to divert his attention. Between turtle-neck and skirt is an exposed half inch of soft cocoa skin. He lasers into it, left hand working away in his pants.

Waiting for the money-shot.

Ten minutes into the movie she gives it to him. She arches her back and her breasts stick out. The turtleneck rides to reveal the caramel smoothness of her belly. (A shiver of revulsion passes down the back of Liam Feegan's neck when he hears the whispered words "work it ... work it..." and he thinks to himself Never. Sit. In Front. Of The Doc.) Then she looks idly round the class and their eyes meet.

The Doc may not be the only boy in the room not watching the screen – an etherised Steve is staring wide-eyed at the ceiling and a couple of others have fallen asleep – but he is the only one staring at Ms Rene. And he doesn't look away. Their eyes lock for a very long time; six whole seconds maybe.

Don't look in my eyes, bitch.

She breaks first.

That's right.

The corners of her mouth tighten. She looks back at the screen.

The Doc wonders if it's possible she doesn't realize what's going on. Can you really not know when someone is staring directly into your eyes that that person is jerking off over you? The Doc doesn't think so. He doesn't think that's possible at all. In fact, he thinks she might like it. He'll even say it, very quietly, like an echo in the ear of a madman, *You like it, don't you Miss? You like it, you filthy little whore – you want me to work that fat ass, don't you? You fuckin' dirty cunt, you fuckin' whore - you like it when I pull up your skirt and stick it in your pussy. You like my rocket cock; you want my rocket cock inside you, dontcha Miss? You want me to fuck you – you want me to fuck you in the ass – you want my big cock – you want it in your ass. I love your sweet ass. I love fucking your sweet ass... I love your... I love you...*

He comes in his boxers. His impeccable command of his facial muscles ensures that the only physiognomic indication is a slight parting of his lips. His senses rush back to him. His breathing suddenly sounds very heavy and loud and he worries about the others hearing him, copping what he's done. But a quick scan of the room confirms that they're all oblivious, or at least acting oblivious. Everyone watches the movie.

The Doc relaxes and looks at the screen. He's not thinking about what's going on in the movie. Not the movie on the screen anyway. He's thinking about the movie he's starting to live through. And about how maybe all it takes is a little balls, a little follow through on all the crazy shit that happens in his head. About how you can take the starring role if you just go for it.

If you really work it.

The bell for the end of class sounds and Ms Rene darts for the TV with unusual haste and turns it off. The Doc's heart skips a beat. He prepares himself to be called out and publicly shamed.

"I think," says Ms Rene, not looking at anyone, "we can have a short day. We'll finish the movie after the Christmas break if that's okay. So you're all free to go. I'll let the headmaster know I've let you out early. Joyeux Noel."

Is that all you'll tell the headmaster, Ms Rene? You won't tell him that one of your boys jerked off over you, now will you? And that you let him?

She grabs her leather satchel and swiftly leaves the room.

14

Great excitement and scurrying to gather books and bags now that the school day has been unexpectedly cut short.

The Doc replaces his foolscap pad and pen in his briefcase and spins the wheels on the lock. The events of the last few minutes have pretty much passed out of his mind. He's already changed the channel. His main concern now is what to do in order to delay going home. He needs an entertainment.

Oversized and under-coordinated Mark is falling over himself to get away from the class room before the Doc can devise some new torment or resurrect an old reliable. The Doc can smell the fear. He skips around the emptying desks and catches Mark by the elbow.

"Hey Mark."

Mark glares at him with suspicion and loathing, shrugging away his elbow.

"I'm not in the mood, Feely, I'm really not in the mood..."

"Not in the mood for what, Mark? For a full and unconditional apology?"

"Seriously Feely, I'll fuckin' drop you..."

"Now Mark, please. Let's be realistic. I only came over to commiserate with you. Over my offences, you know. I traversed, Mark, I traversed a line back there in P.E. And I'm sorry. It's nothing personal. I was just buzzing off you."

"Yeah, well, it doesn't make you less of an asshole, like."

"Well hey now Mark, you can accept my sincere and forthwith apology or you can fuckin'... do whatever you like with it, but there it is."

"Yeah, well, whatever. Just ... don't fuckin' start on me again. I'm serious."

"Okay, okay."

The Doc sticks out his hand for the presidential shake, grasping both Mark's hand and his elbow and pumping vigorously. Mark grudgingly assents and then pulls his arm away and goes for the door.

"Happy Holidays, Mark!"

Mark half-turns and nods, still on his guard. The Doc notes

with satisfaction the snail trail of semen on his elbow.

Steve is the last one left in the class. His face is dark, and purple spots are in full cardiac arrest bloom on his cheeks. He devoted three long and woozy hours between the start of Biology and the end of lunch to hoovering up knockout quantities of ether. There were a lot of laughs. But all he has to show for it now is a bruised tomato complexion and a brain that feels like it's being beaten by a brick. Even the act of looking hurts. He can't look up, he can't look down, he can't even close his eyes without pain. Now the Doc looms over him, one more unendurable pain on the vertical axis. There is no escape. And then the unendurable pain starts speaking to him.

"You got any more wacky sniff-sniff, Stevie-boy?"

Steve's voice whispers to the Doc from some unfathomable private hell.

"Pleeze," he says, "Kill me."

"Don't be such a pussy Steve. I know you're only trying to hold out on me".

"Nooo, Doc. Pleeeze, just kill me." Even on the cusp of death Steve's voice has a giggly tremor beyond his control.

The Doc cocks his head and narrows his eyes, as though seriously considering whether or not to put Steve out of his misery. Then he gets back to the matter in hand. "Ether, Stevie. Hand it over."

"Nooo, no more ether..."

"That's right, no more ether for Steve..."

"No more ether, no more ether..."

"Ether for the Doctor. Come on, hand it over buddy."

"Nooo..."

Debilitated though he is, Steve manages to slide out of his chair. He falls limply against the Doc and stumbles into a semi-upright position. Then he staggers out the door, propelled by a crude primal urge to protect his last reserves of ether, knowing only that, however rough the ride, there yet remained dark territories of brain damage that only Steve deserved to navigate. But the Doc will be damned if he's going to let his quick fix of the moment slip away without a tussle. He follows his beleagured quarry at a distance. Steve is having trouble finding his feet to make a quick get-away. He runs on spasticated legs, grazing and spinning off the walls.

"Where you goin' Stevie?" the Doc calls, his tone expressing utter bafflement that Steve might not want to partake of his company. Steve picks up the pace, accelerating to a fast lurch. The Doc starts loping after him, matching Steve's speed. The sound of the boating shoes slapping the tiles spurs Steve on, sheer blind panic galvanising his wretched limbs into a broken puppet approximation of a sprint. He explodes like a human firework out of the corridor into the main foyer of Xavier. Two seconds later the Doc appears, his crazy legs pumping away at terrifying speeds, doo-doo-doodling the Big Top tune through a cartoon grin.

At the far end of the school, the other sixth year double French class has also finished up early. Twenty green jumpers are on their way to the common room when they hear Steve's unmistakable high pitched screams. Sensing a fight or an entertainment they hurry towards the foyer.

The first of the group to see the cause of the commotion is Bob, who automatically mouths the word 'offensive' as he sees the Doc jumping up and down to either side of Steve and wind-milling the briefcase over his head. Then the briefcase comes down, the flat of it percussing against Steve's back once, twice, thrice, and the Doc burbling in his demented-retarded clown voice, "Don't hold out on me, Stevie boy! You'll never make it into my Crystal Sky Palace that way! Give it up to the Doctor!"

Perhaps the Doc is all of a sudden aware that an audience has gathered and those finely-honed performance instincts of his demand that the routine step up a gear, or perhaps he was just going to do it anyway, but on the fourth swing he twists the briefcase mid-air and aims the corner into the small of Steve's back. Twenty assembled sets of back muscles clench simultaneous with the strike, which hits Steve like a massive electrical surge, snap-curving his spine into a tortured bow.

As Steve writhes beneath him like a cracked fish, the Doc spreads his arms and grins to his audience, expecting applause. Instead he catches Houghton's full shoulder spear tackle right in the gut.

Houghton has been waiting to deliver such a tackle for five years now; five years of general and Doc-specific rage, five years of Fucking Hating the Doc's smart-ass, faggy, pretentious gibberish (gibberish which Houghton has always suspected, with the manly-man's fear of invention and subversion, has been somehow at his expense). And of course, before Houghton bagged Laura she and the Doc had spent that single fateful evening locked in what passion Houghton dare not contemplate; an evening the Doc has never forgiven Laura for, and Houghton has never forgiven either of them for. The tackle Houghton delivers to the Doc's main digestive organs is thus invested with a substantial chronicle of fury. The Doc jack-knifes backwards three feet clear of the prostrate Steve. Houghton pins him and swings wildly at the Doc's face and ribs.

The Doc is terrified by the sheer physical intimacy of big, burly, rugby-playing Houghton lying on him, touching him, breathing on him. He pushes Houghton up and away from him and then launches a kick at his leg. The kick harmlessly grazes Houghton's hip and he returns the favour five-fold. The Doc can only curl up and take it.

Now it's Houghton's turn to stand triumphant over his cowed and foetal opponent. He's puffed out but still plenty able to sermonise. Everything about Houghton right now says, Don't back-talk me if you want to keep your teeth.

"What the fuck is your problem, Feely?"

Well at the moment it pretty much boils down to you, you angry cunt...

"Are you just fuckin' retarded? I mean is that it; is it fuckin' brain-damage?"

I might be if have to listen to you for too long.

"Do you have any idea how much of a fuckin' offensive prick you really are?"

Right back at you, big guy...

"Seriously, do you?"

As I already said...

"Answer me!"

"Look, Howie, I'm sorry..."

"Don't fuckin' apologise to me you stupid cunt! Do you not even see that Steve can hardly stand up?"

"Well, like, I'm sorry, Steve..."

"No one gives a shit if you're sorry, Feely!" screams Houghton. "No one cares what you say! No on one wants to listen to your bullshit! No one listens to you anyway! Do you not fuckin' get it? No one fuckin' likes you! You haven't got any friends, Feely! You think you're such a funny, crazy guy but you're just a fuckin' obnoxious cunt!"

A flat bass-baritone rumbles from the back of the crowd.

"Nobody likes you, Feely," says Mark.

The Doc can take it – has to take it – from Houghton; but Mark is a different story.

"Aw, you got game now, White-Boy?!" he screeches from the floor. "What you gonna do, Mark? Are you gonna SLAM DUNK me? You fuckin' loser," pushing himself up only to be palm-slapped down again by Houghton. The Doc is caught in an anxious space between rage and fear.

"For fuck's sake, Houghton, we were only having a laugh, so

I went a bit too far, I didn't mean..."

"YOU ALWAYS GO TOO FAR YOU FUCKING PSYCHO – well here, I'm just having a laugh, see if you think this is funny," says Houghton. And then he spits in the Doc's face.

The Doc doesn't react. His first thought is, *Well, this is new.* He wipes a foamy smear of saliva off a lens. And then Mark spits in his face.

And then 'Handsome' Brian spits in his face.

And then Benno spits in his face.

And then Houghton spits in his face again.

And then he can't make out who's spitting in his face but more of them are joining in. Maybe all of them. And he just sits there on the ground, the spit accreting like a wet mask. And then he thinks, not just thinks but really knows, *They really hate me*, and he also knows there's nothing he can do about it, and he feels the full weight of all that concentrated hatred pressing down on him so he's not even sure he'll be able to stand up when he tries. And he's almost happy that his face is a mask of spit because he thinks he might be crying and at least with all the spit they won't be able to see it.

"Hey Doc!" shouts Houghton.

Houghton has the Doc's briefcase, his beloved briefcase, and he picks up one of the low benches that line the corridors of Xavier, lifts it over his head, and slams it down. One of the metal legs smashes through the leather-over-plastic siding.

Everyone in the school knows the Doc's briefcase. And Houghton, in a moment of frenzied inspiration, has figured out that putting a hole in the Doc's briefcase is the next best thing to putting a hole in the Doc. Houghton lifts the bench leg out of the briefcase and kicks it across the smooth wooden floor at the Doc. It flips open on the way; the flimsy lock juddered apart by the force of the blow, revealing the paltry contents; two pens, some scrumpled tinfoil from an old sandwich, a foolscap pad, and the Doc's precious copy of *American Psycho.* The Doc has always ensured that its spine remains flawless and unbroken, and its covers and pages unmarred by grease or coffee stains or finger sweat – and now on the cover the picture of Bateman's face is gouged out and the whole book is twisted up from the impact.

"What's wrong, Feely?" says Houghton, "I thought you'd find that pretty funny? We were just, like, having a laugh."

The Doc doesn't hear him. He blows some of the spit out of his mouth and stands, and picks up his briefcase like it's a dead child. He tries to close it over but the lock is out of alignment and it won't click shut, so he holds it against his chest. He glares at the distant, spit smeared images of his school mates and draws in breath.

Fuck you guys. You fucking nobodies, you nothings, you useless, BORING cocksuckers. I wipe my ass of you shit stains.

But nothing comes out. All his verve and rage is sucked down into a big empty hole in his stomach.

Without the usual edge in his voice, Bob says, "Why don't you go home, Doc."

The Doc finally wipes his face with his sleeve and is about to muster a 'Fuck you too, Bob,' when he sees Ms Rene. She's far down the corridor, probably on her way from the staff room. She stands there, looking at him. He wonders how long she's been standing down there. He wonders if she saw the kicking and the spitting and the destruction of his briefcase and he wonders if she deliberately chose not to intervene. And he wants to say sorry to her. But how the hell would that apology go?

So he goes, kicking wide the two sets of swing doors that lead outside.

When he's outside in the chill air he starts running, faster and faster, round the side passage, past the tennis courts and the skips. As he passes the skips he screams an unearthly scream, a scream that carries to everyone in the entire school (and some of them think, *Jesus, who died*?), and flings the ruined briefcase in a high arc. It opens mid-air, and the pens and the torn copy of American Psycho and the foolscap pad and the scrumpled tinfoil float free, and everything bar the foolscap pad lands in the skip.

Houghton jogs as far as the tennis courts and slows to a walk. He hadn't expected Doc to react quite so explosively to a few smacks, and he feels a tiny pang of guilt watching him legging it out the back gate, covered in spit and shame. He sneaks a glance into the skip at the Doc's miserable possessions and then picks up the foolscap pad from the ground and flicks through it. The pages are covered in doodles of dogs and clowns, and scraps of writing that might be movie scripts. As he flicks, the name 'Laura' snags his attention and he takes a closer look at the page. His own name is written above Laura's, along with the names of other people from his year. The page is headed 'Death List'.

Without looking back, the Doc keeps on running, past Tony the janitor who has just unlocked the back gate (and who never ceases to be amazed by the naked emotionalism of Xavier's privileged young men) and into the back streets of Ranelagh. After five hundred yards he slows to a trot, then a walk, then a stagger, his lungs burning from the December air. He forges ahead, glaring at the pavement, until he reaches the bench at the top of Beechwood Avenue.

He sits down and cleans his face with his sleeve as best he can. He leans forward, head in hands, elbows on knees. And then, with the darkness closing in, for today is the second shortest day of the year, a light breaks through; a pack of Benson and Hedges lies beneath the bench, with five cigarettes left. He lights up a cigarette and sits there, smoking and shivering, bleeding pity and hate, waiting for Duke to come home.

15

News of the Doc's disgrace spreads around the school like a toxic fog. Duke finds himself straying into pockets of evil vapour, ill-wind conversations about the misdeeds and mis-sayings of the Doc. No one (apart from Houghton) owns up to having spat in the Doc's face, but the general consensus is that it had been About Time Somebody Stepped Up.

Everyone has beef. The Doc said this to me, the Doc did that to me, he's lost the plot, he's gone off the rails, he practically broke Steve's back AND he tried to basically murder Benno in the yard, yeah, seriously, ask Turk, and Feegan said he was jerking off in French class, the sick fuck, I mean, okay, it's Ms Rene, who hasn't? – *at home*, not in the middle of *class*, with, like, thirty other guys around you, that's just fuckin' rotten, Yeah, no, absolutely, repressed homo all the way, I mean he's a complete psycho, he's just, like, such an Offensive Prick.

None of what people were saying sounded doubt-worthy, arguable or even particularly exaggerated. Yes, the Doc had strayed into attempted murder territory out in the yard, even if malice aforethought would be difficult to establish – thought itself would be difficult to establish; and yes, judging from Steve's appearance and anti-Doc grumblings down in the common room, Steve who was usually such a happy-go-lucky glutton for punishment, it did look like the Doc had worked him over with especial vigour. And yes, the Doc had been threatening public masturbation for so long there was nothing inconsistent about the Ms Rene story. And yes, the Doc was, from the Brylcreem sheen of his executive do to the smooth white tips of his ridiculous boating shoes, a singularly offensive character, even before he opened his mouth. And when he opened his mouth… As last remaining friend of the Doc, Duke can sense the magnetic field of social proscription making large, empty spaces around him. He likes to believe that that sort of shit doesn't really bother him. But it does. He clears out of Xavier.

On the walk home he thinks about the evening ahead. He figures there's lots of fun things a social pariah can get up to on a Friday night and is listing them off in his head when he sees the Doc sitting on the bench at the top of Beechwood Avenue.

Of course he's here. Where else would he go?

Half-hoping the Doc will pick up on his body language from this distance, Duke sighs heavily, his anticipation of a few unmolested hours vapouring into the air with his haw breath. Already at ten to four there are only a few minutes of light left before the gloaming. Duke walks in and out of the illuminated stretches where the sun shoots between the houses, his shadow thirty feet long. He keeps his head lowered to avoid extended long-distance eye contact with the Doc. Even when he gets to the bench and sits down Duke makes no outward sign of acknowledgement. Neither does the Doc.

They sit awhile in silence. Duke, not normally a smoker, takes a cigarette from the pack of Benson that lies between them. The Doc lights it without needing to be asked.

It's almost nice, thinks Duke. *Sharing a melancholy moment, two boy-men together on a bench, taking a breather from the relentless Alfred Jarry antics for a short Beckettian interlude. Two boy-men on a bench, side by side in the gathering gloom, sunk in who knows what profounds of mind, of...*

"I fucked a hooker last night."

Or not.

The Doc stares straight ahead when he speaks. Duke adopts the same tactic for listening to him. A scene from The Silence of the Lambs flits through Duke's mind, the one where Hannibal Lector tells Clarice to describe some awful childhood episode. Lector turns his back to her so he can hear her voice clearly and without the distraction of a face. Lector's line is "Don't lie to me. I'll know." Duke gives the Doc a silence to fill. The Doc obliges.

"Near the Burlo. That street by Annabel's."

The Doc's voice is tired. Duke can tell he isn't really up to this.

"There was another beat down dog on Fitzwilliam Square but you wouldn't go near it. So I walked up to Leeson Street and there she was. Blonde. Looked a bit like Laura."

Here we go again...

"I didn't even realise she was a hooker. I mean she was just dressed all normally, you know, like a normal girl. So I go up to talk to her and, like, it's pretty obvious she's a hooker when we get talking but she's a nice girl – anyway, suddenly she starts acting all dirty, like, you know, pressing herself against me and then, like, she grabs my cock through my pants and starts telling me that she'll give me a suck and we can negotiate the price later. I mean, it should have been obvious that I don't have any money but I guess maybe she thinks I do – or maybe she's just lonely or something, I don't know, I mean I guess there aren't many guys looking for a shivering rained-on little hooker at three o'clock in the morning..."

I'd say there are plenty of guys looking for a shivering, rained-on little hooker at three o'clock in the morning but whatever; it's your made-up story...

"And then she, like, starts pulling me by my belt buckle into an alley and unzipping my fly..."

Hold on. Were you wearing a belt last night? I don't think you were. Poor detailing, Doc...

"And it takes her ages because, well, you know how those pants are pretty ass-hugging and it's freezing wet so I'm turtling like a fuckin' faggot..."

Good detailing, the vulnerable touch, I like it...

"But she gets it open and she roots around and like I'm afraid she's going to laugh at it because there's only about half an inch of cock flesh on show when she gets through my boxers but I swear to God she starts sucking on it for, like. Ages. And finally I get a hard-on. It's fuckin' crazy; I mean I think it was still raining or sleeting or whatever and here's this beautiful girl squatting on the ground and sucking my cock in the middle of the road..."

"I thought you said 'alley'?"

"Yeah, like, alley, middle of the road, it's a fuckin' figure of speech. The point is she's going down on me. In the street."

The Doc stops talking. Duke remains impassive.

Does he expect me to believe any of this shit, he wonders. *Is it enough that I'm just here? Do I even need to be here? Ah, now, hold on a sec, he's your friend, he's in trouble. Be a friend...*

Duke registers the Doc's eyes flicking momentarily to his face.

"I didn't come anyway," he says, his voice thick with pathos. "It's not like it was a bad blow-job or anything. I mean it was pretty good as blow-jobs go. Maybe her mouth was too small or something..."

Sure it was...

"I don't know. I don't really have much experience you know."

He pauses. Then – "Yeah, that was my first time," he says curtly, matter-of-fact.

Alright! Alright, you demented bastard, you win! My heart is a quiverful of arrows, the violins are swelling, this obviously means a lot to you so if you really want to keep on shovelling I'll just have keep right on swallowing...

"Jesus, Doc. Sounds like a hell of a night you had there," says Duke, his trusty demon cynicism exorcised from his tone so thoroughly it's almost suspicious.

The Doc is eager to engage in confidence-sharing now.

"Yeah, it was heavy stuff. Intense..."

Intensely made-up maybe...

"I mean I don't know if you knew I was, you know, like, emm, inexperienced..."

"A virgin?"

"Yeah, well, like yeah, whatever. I'm glad I'm not now though. It wasn't even that good, but ... it's a relief ... not to be..."

Now you really are breaking my heart...

"It's not there weren't opportunities before. I practically fucked Laura that time in Julian's gaff..."

No. No you didn't. Did you?

"But she was too chickenshit. That's why Houghton's always had such a hard-on for me, 'cause I nearly fucked his precious bitch girlfriend...."

"What about your own hard-on, Doc?" says Duke, not wanting to get wrangled into old war stories or new.

"What?"

"After your run-in with the young mistress of the night. Who ended up bearing the brunt of your ithyphallic state? Is Doogie wandering around your house trickling blood by any chance?"

"Doogie? How can you say such things? My love for Doogie is pure. I went back to that hotel we foamed up. The foam was all gone with the rain and all. So I broke into this janitor's closet style place and found a copy of *Good Housekeeping* and had a wank in the jacks."

Duke laughs. *This is more like it*, he thinks.

"*Good Housekeeping*?"

"I was thinking of your mum."

"You and everyone else. So you got a blow-job from a prostitute, broke into a hotel and jerked off in a janitor's closet. Good thing I left when I did."

"Oh yeah. Did you get up to anything after you pussied off and left me?"

Duke considers telling him about the strange and dramatic events in Bob's place and decides it'll only make the Doc feel even more left out.

"Nope. Just went home."

Duke stands suddenly and the Doc follows suit. The last rays have slunk off over the horizon and somehow it's night, or a least the street-lamp orange that passes for night in these parts.

They walk for a short time without saying anything, both of them internally scrambling for a new subject to defray potential inquiries regarding the Doc's recent humiliation. The Doc hits on one. "I had another clown dream last night," he says, immediately perking up at the thought. The Doc is quite proud of his clown dreams.

"Anything new to report?" says Duke.

Duke, constitutionally inclined to the appreciation of dreams, is always an engaged listener.

"Bateman was there," says the Doc, his eyes sparkling at the remembrance, "but I couldn't hear him or see him properly. I think I was going to stab him but I couldn't get the knife to work."

"Ahh," says Duke, "flaccid blade syndrome."

"Who's flaccid?"

"No one. Go on."

"Alright. Are you sure you aren't calling me a faggot?"

"Positive."

"Alright. So Bateman is changing into something and I run away. And I'm running through these blocks of skyscrapers. And then the three legged clown is behind me..."

"Hold on. The clown has three legs?"

"Yeah."

"You never told me he had three legs."

"Well, he does. Anyway, I can hear his huge clown shoes pounding the pavement. And I keep catching glimpses of his crazy clown face in the windows of the skyscrapers."

"Has he always had three legs?"

"Yes, he's always had three legs!"

"Fascinating. What colour are his shoes?"

"What do you mean what colour are his shoes? They're clown shoes. They're big and red and shiny."

"Doc, I'm gonna stop you there. And I'm going to have to retract my earlier reassurance that you're not a faggot. This is one of the gayest dreams that's ever been brought to my attention."

"Bullshit!"

"I'm afraid not. Think about it. This 'huge' clown has three legs. Three legs, Doc. Entailing a supernumery middle appendage of grotesque proportions ending in an enormous, shiny red bell-end."

"What's your point?"

"It's a cock, Doc!"

"No! No, you're not allowed do this..."

"It's already done. You can't argue with phallic symbolism."

"This is just your psychoanalysis bullshit."

"Well, that's dreams for you. The cock is beyond contention. What we need to figure out now is – what are the larger ramifications of the clown dream? For your gayness, that is."

"No. Bollocks. This isn't allowed. I've told you about this."

"The clown is running after you, yes? And you always wake up before he tramples you, yes? Now what do you think would happen if you, just the one time, let the clown run over you?" says Duke, raising an eyebrow. "Do you think you'd like it?"

"Stop now, I swear to God, just... stop it, Dookey. I'm warning you..."

"Face facts, Doc. You want this clown to fuck you in the ass."

"I don't want anything near my ass!"

"Okay, well we'll leave that aside for a minute... but you're not so shy about other people's asses, are you? And I know it's supposed to be in jest, but you do dry hump a lot of men. I reckon anyone who wants to give it so much probably wants to take it too. In the ass, I mean. Doc," says Duke, his face creased with concern and sympathy, "I'm sorry, I really am – but you're a clearly a flaming homo." By way of response, Doc starts humping Duke ferociously, catching him sideways and giving his left hip the full doggy action. Duke tries to remain unruffled despite this onslaught of crotch.

"Doc, this isn't helping your case. See reason. You won't get any satisfaction by humping a fully-fledged heterosexual like myself."

The Doc redoubles his efforts.

"You need to be among your own kind."

Duke can sense the Doc trying to sneakily force an advantage, attempting to assert some kind of compensatory dominance. It's there in the strain of his arm muscles and the way he's trying to force an unspoken surrender. So Duke decides to push back.

To test you. See what the Doc's got in reserve.

They're right outside Duke's house now, grappling in the tiny city-mews garden. There isn't room to swing a cat, much less a full-grown Doc, but that's what Duke tries to do. The Doc has almost succeeded in manoeuvring him into the supplicant position. Duke tenses against him.

Duke knows that in any test of strength between evenly matched competitors the trick is to anticipate the strike. Muscle will be tensed against muscle at a latent point; in order to force an advantage one party has to tense further. But between the latent stage and the pressing for advantage is a very slight but unavoidable relaxation. The trick, therefore, is to anticipate this brief lessening of tension in your opponent and effect a counter strike in the brief interim. It's less than the blink of an eye. But Duke can hear when the Doc is going to go for gold. He snaps back against him and pushes him far enough away to turn face to face. For a moment their eyes meet. An unspoken question seems to penetrate first Doc's gaze, and then Duke's, but then fades as quickly as it came.

They grab each other either side of their necks, both tired already, locked in a bull's horn stalemate. They describe small circles on Duke's lawn, testing each other with little feints and pushes, strange smiles on their faces, smiles that say (a little too forcefully) 'aren't we having fun'.

"You shee theesh bootsh," says the Doc. It's his bald neo-Nazi from *Falling Down* voice. "Good for shtompin' faggots. Problem is you get all the faggot waffle stuck in 'em."

Duke smiles thinly. "There's only one fag around here, Doc. The subconscious doesn't lie."

The Doc drops the voice. "Stop calling me a fag, Dookey."

"Stop looking at my ass then," says Duke, thinking this is a very funny line. The Doc smiles back at him, showing all his teeth.

"You're such a funny fucker, Dookey," he says, and with an impulse of shocking strength manages to lift and twist Duke by the shoulders and slam him on the ground. He pins him.

"You're just *sooooo fun-ny.*"

Now his hands close around Duke's throat. The Joker smile never wavers. It's like a mask. There's steel in his voice now, and behind the steel something frantic and pleading.

"I *don't* want to fuck other men in the ass, Dookey. D'you understand? That's you. You're the ass-fucker, Dookey. You and Houghton and all the rest of those ass-fuckers."

His hands are worryingly constrictive now and for pretty much the first time ever Duke wonders very seriously if the Doc could actually make good on his homicidal mutterings and routines.

"And you think you're so fucking smart, Dookey. You think you've got me all figured out but it's all bullshit, it's all just psycho-babble bullshit, you haven't got a fucking clue."

And Duke is thinking *Jesus, this is sad. He really does want to kill me. And I'm his best friend. I'm his only friend.*

"You don't know me. You don't know where I've been, maaaaan!"

And now he's just quoting from the movies! Who the hell does he think he's performing for? Does he think I'm going to stand up and applaud if I blackout and die? Does he know this is real? Does he get that?

"Well I'm not gonna take it anymore, Dookey! You hear me? I'm mad as hell and I'm not going to take it any more! Things is gonna change round here!"

Never a director around when you need one.

Duke stares into the Doc's eyes like he's just caught the perfect shot and with the breath left in his throat manages to hiss the single word; "Cut!" It's an audacious move but the context has become so weird and fabricated, and the Doc's reality filters so warped, that he thinks it might just work. He thinks it damn well better work. And it does.

The hands unknit themselves from his throat. The crazed expression melts away. For a second the Doc is completely transparent and there's something like shock or guilt in his eyes, conscience maybe, and for the briefest of earthly moments the Doc believes he's done something wrong. Which is completely different from people telling him he's done something wrong. It's different because he's looking at his best friend, the one he goes to automatically, when the whole of the rest of the world is pointing the finger and showing him the door – and that's fine, that seems to be the natural order, and sometimes its worse than other times, but it's okay for the rest of the world to lock him out, he expects that, just so long as there's one other person inhabiting the Doc's own world, and that person is Dukey. And if Dukey locks him out then there's only the other shitty world that wants nothing to do with the Doc. Some such wordless surge of feeling flickers momentarily in his eyes. And then it's gone again.

The Doc stands up. As he stands he feigns a slight backwards limp, as though he'd received a hitherto unremarked injury in the course of their grappling. He exhales heavily. He laughs a brittle laugh.

"Good tussle, Dookey. Nearly had me there," he says, raising his arms mock strongman style. "But the Doc is triumphant." He sticks out his hand. "Come on Dookey, you'll get piles lying on the ground like that."

I guess this is as good as it gets.

Duke lets himself be hoisted up, not yet willing to look the Doc in the eye, not yet willing to let him off the hook. Under an evil silence he fumbles for his house keys, finds them and opens the front door. He takes two steps into the hallway.

"You coming in?"

The Doc moseys in after him.

Jesus, I really am the girl in this relationship, thinks Duke. He is already considering what comestibles he might be able to rustle up for his ever ravenous charge.

The kitchen is busy with traces of his mum. New magazines on the couch, the flyers and free postcards she picks up everywhere, fresh flowers in a vase on the kitchen table and a pan of nutty looking risotto on the stove.

Duke turns on the hob to heat the risotto and fumbles around for nibbles. The Doc is doing his usual trick of flicking through the magazines. Current affairs, literature, art; they were all outside the Doc's hopelessly narrow sphere of interest. He was just flicking for the sake of flicking.

"Sit," says Duke, and the Doc sits.

Duke broods over the risotto, spicing it up with whatever condiments catch his eye. He serves up generously and even gives the Doc a beer from the fridge. They sip their beer and eat their food without speaking until the Doc asks to see his letter. Duke obliges and the Doc reads aloud, laughing at his malevolent inventions. Duke doesn't join in. When the Doc gets to the bit about drawing headless women in vomit he explodes with glee at the rottenness of his imagination.

"Enjoying that, are you?" says Duke.

"I'm a fucking genius! This may be my premier superwork!"

Duke shrugs.

"What?" says the Doc. "This is hilarious. You love this shit."

"Oh yeah, no it's fine. It's just… well you know yourself, it's not exactly literature."

Duke keeps his manner off-hand while scouring the table for he knows not quite what before settling for the last dregs of his beer.

"Well," he says, "I suppose you'll be going home then?"

For once, the Doc takes the hint. He hesitates, then places the letter carefully on the table.

"Yeah. Yeah, I guess I better head."

The Doc casts about for his belongings, realises he doesn't have any and stands up from the table. Duke walks him to the door.

"Have you got your briefcase?" says Duke, assuming its presence. The Doc looks momentarily panicked.

"Oh, yeah. No, I don't. Fucked it in a skip."

Duke just nods as though the matter has been settled to everyone's satisfaction and leads the Doc out. Doc looks so sad that he has to throw him some small token of rapprochement.

"Might see you at Julian's tomorrow night then?"

The Doc looks at him blankly.

So they managed to hide that from you, eh? thinks Duke, pretending not to notice.

"Should be a good party," says Duke.

"Oh yeah, nearly forgot about that," says the Doc. "Well, catch you later, Dookey."

"Later, Doc."

The Doc walks to the gate and Duke shuts the door. The gate hinges squeal and then clang.

Duke potters around the kitchen cleaning up, feeling alternately sorry for the Doc and then annoyed that the Doc can make him feel sorry. He scrapes the remains of the risotto into the bin and scrubs the plates, talking to himself.

I cook for him, I clean for him…

He gathers the magazines and makes a neat stack on the coffee table.

I educate him, or God knows I try…

He brings the letter up to his bedroom and files it away in his correspondence chest.

I'm a willing audience for his rants; I even offer constructive criticism…

He wanders back downstairs and slumps into an armchair, dog-tired.

In a word, I play the dutiful wifey just short of allowing him to stick his stubby frustrated little member into me – and what do I get in return? Guilt trips and attempted murder.

He sits in the armchair awhile, letting his thoughts play out on the blank black of the dormant TV screen. Then he sees something in the squashed, curved reflection that nearly kills him. His limbs are suddenly afraid to move. The side of his face in view of the living room window feels hot and prickly.

After a measured count to ten he stands up and strolls over to the bookshelves. His fingers meander along the spines of the glossy art-books and pick one out at random. He opens the book of Miro prints and walks over to the light dial, his eyes never leaving the brightly coloured smiley faces on the page. Then he turns the lights up full, as though to see the prints better. He holds his breath and walks to the window with its wooden Venetian blinds.

Duke knows that with all the lights on inside the room, and the close blackness outside, it would be perfectly conceivable that all he'd be able to see in the window would be his own reflection. He knows that by not letting his eyes focus on any point beyond the glass that no one could accuse him of knowingly over-looking the twin rectangular panes of the Doc's D&Gs, brightly glaring in the blackness and obscurely attached to the milky grayness of the Doc's face. Duke reckons he was cleaning up for the best part of twenty minutes. Which means that the Doc has been standing outside the window for a very long time, waiting for Duke to notice him. All Duke has to do is see the Doc and act surprised. That's all it would take on Duke's part to play the game to its end.

But playtime's over, thinks Duke.

As Duke pulls the drawstring that shutters the slats he is outside with the Doc, looking through the Doc's eyes, and he sees the transverse rows of light winking out and he sees himself disappearing from view.

16

Doc walks home. He has walked this way a thousand times. He walks through Ranelagh and Closkeagh and then into Dundrum and beyond to the less fashionable suburbs, where he lives. He walks with the flow of people who are returning home from work. He walks against the flow of people already heading into town.

Fuck them, he says to himself. *Fuck them and fuck Duke and fuck the school and fuck them all.*

The Doc knows how helpless they all are. He really *knows*. He knows the way Bateman would know. He can see Bateman stalking through these complacent ranks, and the Doc can feel it in his limbs; the power, the control... and then... and then he sees a three legged clown pounding up the streets, his perma-grin balloon head thrust back by his awesome velocity, his lunatic eyes sightlessly heaven-bound, oblivious to the pulpy, yowling mess of pedestrians ground into chum beneath his feet...

The Doc alone is haughty and proud, beholden to nothing and no one. And this mood of glorious isolation or insulation or Crystal Sky Palace observation lasts all the way home, and all the way through the front door of the dismal house, and up the stairs, and into the bathroom, and while he takes a piss and washes his hands and goes back down the stairs and into the kitchen. And when he opens the kitchen door he sees his hated brother neck-deep in the fridge – and he sees his frazzled mum by the oven – and he sees the old man in front of the TV – and he sees Doogie licking the wall – the whole clan, as real as real can be, the realest group of bodies in the world. Doc senses something contrived in the atmosphere. Something staged. His family are never found congregating in the same room. The house is large enough to grant all four inhabitants their separate zones of activity and reduce interaction to the bare minimum; grimly crab-stepping past each other on the stairs, shocked rattles at the bathroom's door-handle, that sort of thing. Mrs Feely, nervous, brow-beaten and almost crazed with isolation, would doubtless prefer some sense of 'family' over the prevailing atmosphere of begrudging cohabitation. The three men, however, are perfectly content with this arrangement. The three men rule the roost. So the presence of everyone in the same place strikes the Doc as a very conspicuous happenstance indeed. Conspicuous and planned. The Doc sees them together and thinks, *What have I done? What do they know?*

Tom's dead eyes slowly register the Doc as he folds a slice of processed ham into his mouth. Tom chews the watery meat, still looking at the Doc, and opens his mouth at his younger brother. *This is what I think of you*, say the dead eyes over the open mouth baring the masticated meat. Mrs Feely stands further down the kitchen, tending to a baking tray of chicken and roast potatoes, pouring over the juice. She looks up briefly and makes a helpless gesture of all-consuming busyness, occupied as she is by the baking tray and a single saucepan. Mr Feely sits at the kitchen table watching the TV – tuned to a digital channel devoted to all things nautical. Without shifting his gaze from the pretty schooner on the screen he projects his voice to the frozen Doc in the doorway.

"Well look what the cat dragged in. Just in time to dip your snout in the trough."

The table is neatly laid. The Doc can't get a clear memory of when the family last sat down together for a meal. His mum often cooks a dinner, but everyone always manages to eat their portion at different times to everyone else. He supposes they probably did the communal thing last Christmas, but even that would have been co-incidental chow-down, around the warm and isolating glow of TV. "How was school, hon?" says Mrs Feely, transporting her bustle from the oven to the kitchen table, an impressively hectic movement de-spite the fact that all she does is lay out a last plate.

"Shite," says the Doc, absently.

"Watch your filthy mouth," says his dad, absently.

"Sorry, sir."

"Your mother doesn't appreciate that sort of language."

"No, sir."

"What do you mean 'no'. I said she doesn't appreciate that sort of language. I thought the Jesuits would at least know a double neg-ative when it's up and dressed."

"Yes, sir."

"You're *such. A tard*," says Tom, drawling from the fridge.

"Go back to your pies, dough-boy," says the Doc.

Tom responds by sticking out his tongue and displaying the ham residue again.

"Now," says Mrs Feely, "dinner is served."

"It's not though, is it dear?" says Mr Feely. "It's cooked but it's not actually served, is it?"

Indeed the food, though cooked and ready to be served, is not yet on the table. Mr Feely is a great stickler for exactitude. In response to her husband's mildly threatening pedantry Mrs Feely creases her mouth in self-reproach.

"There seems to be a great deal of linguistic laziness going around today," says Mr Feely, and his sweeping gaze indicts his entire brood on the charge of moral lassitude. He closely observes his wife lay out the chicken (parched, unseasoned), vegetables (boiled, unseasoned), potatoes (roasted, unseasoned) and gravy boat (Bisto, chicken stock, a splodge of ketchup, some very finely sliced scallions and a sneaky pinch of paprika – the gravy is Mrs Feely's sole creative culinary outlet. Mr Feely has firm notions regarding gratuitous seasoning, which means anything more than the salt and pepper he applies himself – but the making of gravy is an arcane, female business and he allows it to happen obscurely and without censure).

"Now," says Mr Feely after making sure the dishes on the table are symmetrically arrayed, "Dinner is served."

"Yeah," says the Doc, still lingering uncomfortably by the door, "I actually already had a bite to eat..."

Mr Feely looks at him.

The Doc sits down.

A carving knife and fork have been set down beside the chicken for Mr Feely to do the honours. This too is an unprecedented novelty. The knife gleams evilly, never before unsheathed from the block. All remain respectfully silent as the patriarch shears ragged hunks of dry white meat off the carcass. It's a savage business; a table-rattling struggle between man and beast. Mr Feely's expression remains sanguine throughout, even when he accidentally cuts right into the spine and lofts the whole chicken high off the serving plate. He knows this is man's work, and that man will triumph in the end.

The Doc looks into his father's face, so detached from the murderous work of his hands, with something like adoration. The sort of adoration due to a wrathful God. When the bird is roughly quartered they all serve themselves; the chef, as is only proper, last and least. Ten minutes of mostly silent eating follow, with occasional and essentially discountable interjections from Mrs Feely: "Isn't this nice?" "I do hope the chicken's okay; it's not too dry is it?" "The chicken's dry isn't it? I left it too long." "I knew I shouldn't have gone to that butcher but you just can't trust Superquinn anymore - the

meat counter's gone to the dogs." "Would anyone like seconds? There's too much for me, I'm really not hungry."
The Doc thinks he can remember family meal times being a regular feature of his childhood. They used to have sophisticated nineties food; chicken Kievs and microwaveable curries from Marks and Spencers. His dad didn't go away on business so much. They seemed to dislike each other a little less. But the Doc realises that his memory may be faulty on this point.

When the last of the gravy is mopped up with the last of the roast potatoes Mr Feely places his knife and fork on the plate, balancing the handle of the knife perpendicular on the handle of the fork and slotting the blade between the tines. Mr Feely derives great solace from just such examples of precarious equilibrium in his life. He addresses his number one son.

"So, Tommy-boy. How's the working life treating you?"

Tom, until recently unemployed and seemingly unemployable, had been given a gofer job by Mr Feely in the mysterious place the Doc knows only as 'the office'. The Doc has never been aware of what his father does for a living, nor has he ever demonstrated an interest. It seems to involve a lot of travelling. Whatever the business consists of its infrastructure is clearly substantial enough to absorb the lumbering incompetence of Tom. The Doc is convinced Tom's responsibilities can't extend beyond scratching himself and bumping into things.

"It's great, Dad. I mean, like you always say, it's easy when your manager doesn't have his head stuck up his ass," says Tom.

Mr Feely guffaws at this choice morsel of reflected wisdom.

"Well," says Mr Feely, wiping a tear from his eye, "you might think better of that in a few weeks, but I'll take that as a compliment, Tommy-boy."

Tom rewards himself for this little work-life/home-life coup by dipping a chicken wing in the gravy boat and sucking it down to the bones.

"It's absolutely true what you say, though," says Mr Feely. "The major impediment to any young man of ability and application is cack-handed management. If you have a clear remit, you understand me, if you know at every minute during the day exactly what your responsibilities are, the work practically does itself."

The Doc imagines his dad handing Tom a list every morning:

1.) Scratch yourself.

2.) Dip your tie in your coffee.

3.) Be a fat lazy moron.

4.) Lunch.

"Yeah, I do actually have to do stuff, Dad," says Tom, sensing that he is being subtly undermined.

"Course you do, Tommy-boy, course you do," says Mr Feely, "I'm not trying to detract from the sweat of your brow or the grease of your elbow. All I'm saying is that because you are clear in your mind about the tasks you are called upon to perform, that you are capable of performing those tasks efficiently. You're not flying blind. The shortcomings of the em-ploy-ee are invariably the shortcomings of the em-ploy-er. And," he continues, at home with his theme now, "I venture that the converse is also true."

"Whatever you say, Dad. You're the boss, right?"

"Right and right again, Tommy-boy," says Mr Feely, chuckling heartily for the second time. The Doc wishes he had the ability to vomit at will.

The agreement of Mr Feely with Mr Feely via the proxy Tom leads to a momentary lull in conversation. The Doc tries to reduce his conspicuousness by redistributing the scraps of broccoli and chicken skin on his plate as though he were considering a final assault on the meal. The ploy does not succeed.

"Well, Number Two son, how was school? In more than a one-word profanity."

Mr Feely maintains that his habit of referring to his progeny by numerical order of birth is a harmless idiosyncrasy, inspired by the rankings system in *Star Trek*. The Doc does not buy this.

"School's fine. 'S grand," says the Doc to his plate.

Mr Feely pulls a surprised face. His eyebrows soar towards his hairline and his mouth upturns beneath the thick black moustache.

"That's all you've got to say for yourself? I spend three thousand a year on that exceptional Jesuit establishment of learning and all you can say is 'Fine. Grand?'"

"All the Jesuits are dead, Dad," says the Doc.

"What? Ludicrous. What about Father Harkin? Or Jim McMasters?"

"Father Harkin is a senile old abuser, dad. And Mr McMaster's isn't a Jesuit. He just lets the parents think he is because he knows it impresses them."

The moustache bristles.

"Maybe I'll have to ask for my money back then. But I somehow doubt the school will refund me. So I suppose I'll just have to get it off you. How much are you into me for now; fifteen, eighteen grand by the end of next year? And that's not including school trips, books, car fare…"

"Yeah, I'll get you back."

Mr Feely snorts dismissively. The Doc realises he has to say something.

"School's school. The people are eejits but what do you expect? The subjects are boring and pointless but it's the same for everyone. I don't know, what do you want me to say?"

Mr Feely is coolly observant. Mrs Feely is worried. Tom is enjoying himself.

"You think you've got it pretty tough, don't you?" says Mr Feely. "You think it's all so unfair. Well it's not. Wait 'til you have to get a job. Wait 'til you have to work for a living."

"James," says Mrs Feely in a cautionary tone. He ignores her.

"You get to faff about, living off my back, and all I get in return is bitching. Little girl bitching."

Tom sniggers into his glass and his orange juice bubbles over the rim onto the tablecloth.

"But I *work* now!" says the Doc. "*For nothing*! I don't even get to make a living!"

Mr Feely mimics him back, his voice an obscene and unsettling approximation of a little girl's, terrifyingly wrong with that face and moustache. "I work now! For nothing! You do in your pie-hole. Where's the grades to prove it? Ever think of that? Maybe if I saw a few A's and B's instead of D's and E's I might be more sympathetic." Tom has been thrown into irrepressible convulsions by the little girl act. His obese frame shakes with gleeful schadenfreude hysterics. "Tom," says Mr Feely, "would you mind leaving us alone with Johnnie for a few minutes?"

Tom's face falls, as though his favourite TV show has been interrupted by a news-flash. Mr Feely's eyes flick to the door. Tom curls his lips at his younger brother and plods out of the kitchen. The Doc half-wishes he wouldn't leave. The scab on his forehead tingles. He feels very … watched. Mr Feely shunts his chair back with a rubbery screech.

"Ronald," says Mrs Feely, "maybe we could…"

"Maybe what?"

Mrs Feely looks guilty for having spoken out of turn. The Doc can't help but be drawn into his mother's aura of paralysed terror. Mr Feely stands up and goes to the corner of the kitchen counter reserved for incoming mail. With his back to the Doc he withdraws something from the small pile of envelopes. Possibilities race through the Doc's mind: an early report card from the Christmas exams, a court summons, those magic mushrooms he and Duke ordered ages ago from an on-line shop in Amsterdam which never came, a letter from someone's parents (*'We found a note in Mark's cold, dead hand describing the abuses one 'The Doc' meted out on a daily basis...'*).

Mr Feely turns. He obscures the offending object, whatever it is, in his huge, hirsute hands, clicking the edge with a fingernail. Mr Feely looks at the Doc and the Doc looks at his father's face, so like his own, the black hair, the squared-off glasses, not actually black but a rich, dark teak, his Roman nose and those piercing eyes beneath the heavy black brows – but his father's face seems so huge, so much larger and realer than the Doc's own face. All the Doc wants now is for his dad to tear up whatever he has in his hands and throw it in the bin and tell the Doc that it doesn't matter, that they'll talk about it some other time...

His dad suddenly flings the terrible thing onto the table, gives it a little wrist action so it spins through the air like the game-winning ace of spades. It slides across the sheer table-top and is about to slide over the edge and onto the Doc's lap before he stops it with a finger. And examines it.

His middle finger is pressed to the oily head of an erect and burnished penis, his fingertip right on the jap's eye, which has been reproduced on the postcard in glossy, high-definition black and white. In the bottom left hand corner is the name '*Robert Mapplethorpe*'. His hand flinches from the photo and he suffers a moment of breathless shock.

This might be the funniest thing that's ever happened to me.

"Ahmm..." says the Doc with convincing bafflement and a shrug of his shoulders, "what's the deal here?"

Mr Feely stands behind Mrs Feely, both hands gripping the back of her chair.

"The. Image," says Mr Feely, "is the least of it."

The Doc's brow creases and he flips the postcard over. On the reverse is a solid block of tiny, handwritten scrawl, so dense as to be almost impenetrable. Obviously not impenetrable enough, though. He reads, and as he reads his mounting anxiety hardens into a tiny ball of solid fear. The postcard begins,

Dear Lovelumps,

Every waking hour is a torment without the succour of your sweet embrace, the oleaginous penetration of your Rocket Cock, the agonising tension of your ballistic balls – invade me with your weapons of mass destruction. I dream of prising apart those cheeky little cheeks with a speculum and jerking off down your brown spout until my semen o'erflows the hole and trickles down your legs, submerging your delicate thigh hairs like mosquitoes in amber, like moths in candle-wax, drawn to the flame of your love. I find myself inspired to create a little poetry –

There followed a paragraph of William Burroughs's style cut-up, all randy cowboys, ejaculations like founts of mercury and the ectoplasmic melding of bodies. The postcard concludes -

Don't you just know how he feels? The Priest, they called him. The Doc, they call you. Non sequitorsville? I think non. I mean not. Dukey. X.

In the bottom right hand corner, beneath the crammed address, Duke had drawn a picture of a hanged man, his delicately suggested phallus indelicately erect and probably spurting, but the perspiring thumb of the Doc has obscured the full nature of the rendering.

The Doc knows without having to look at his reflection in the kitchen window that his face is completely white. He knows that if he were able to stand up he could take a running leap straight through the kitchen window without feeling the glass. But he is not able to stand up. Nor is he able to hide the tremour in his hands. Above all, he is unable to raise his head from the awful words on the table.

To explain away this offensive document, to tease out the nuances of reference, in-jokes, irony, intertextuality, the mixture of saccharine and genuinely menacing homoeroticism, the strange charm of competitive letter-writing, Dukey's fondness for destructive literary stylings – all this is far beyond the Doc's powers of explication or articulation, and far beyond his parents' powers of comprehension or acceptance.

The Doc says, "I know this looks bad…"

"It doesn't *look* bad, Jonathon," says Mr Feely.

"Yeah. No. It is bad. I know."

"So talk to me. Explain."

"It's like," says the Doc, struggling. "It's hard to explain. It's a joke, like."

"This is not a fucking joke! We're treating this matter very fucking seriously!"

"I know, I know..."

"And we expect you to treat it very fucking seriously!"

"I know, I am..."

"So have a little cop-on about the situation!"

"I don't mean the situation is a joke. The postcard's a joke."

"Well, I'm not laughing. And you're mother's not laughing. It's sick, is what it is. You don't send pictures of a fucking... erect phallus... to your friend's family home, you just don't..."

"That's just Dukey, you know? He's a weird guy..."

"He's a malignant little shit is what he is. I've never liked that boy. Your mother's never liked that boy, have you Maureen?"

"No," whispers Mrs Feely.

"There's something off about him. He's a right smart-arse too," says Mr Feely, though he has never actually exchanged a single word with Duke.

"Yes, sir," says the Doc.

"I've never liked that you knock around with him. And I especially don't like him making... repellent intrusions into our home."

"No, sir," says the Doc.

The Doc is attempts to do the only thing he feels he can pull off right now; agree the argument into the ground. There follow several painful and wordless seconds of trenchant parental disapproval and acute filial embarrassment. Mrs Feely, astonishingly, gets the ball rolling again.

"Is there anything you want to talk to us about, Johnny?" she says.

Her voice is inflected with a needling mixture of urgency and concern that sets alarm bells ringing.

"What do you mean?" says the Doc.

"You know what your mother means," says Mr Feely.

The Doc shrugs and shakes his head, even though he does know what his mother means, of course he knows what she means; his mother's worries are as predictable as the rising price of property, the decline of the Catholic Church, drugs are bad for you, money is good for you, and not in my back yard... above all, not in my back yard.

"Some of the things ... he's written," says Mrs Feely. "Some of the... the imagery... the things he says he's like to do to you..."

And the Doc feels so sorry for his mum, so desperately, achingly sorry for the poor nervous bundle his mother has become, or maybe always was, that he could just burst out crying...

"The faggot shit," says Mr Feely. "Your mother won't say it but I will. What's going on, John?"

This last question Mr Feely states bluntly, all accusation and reproach (so he thinks) stripped from his voice. The Doc can only lower his head still further and whisper 'Jesus Christ,' to the floor, and he thinks, Bet you didn't know how much damage you could do with a dirty postcard, Dookey.

Mr Feely exhales, preparing himself for the plunge.

"Are you and this Duke fellah..."

But even the plain-spoken Mr Feely can't bring himself to say the terrible words. The unspoken word sits like a turd between the Doc and his parents, filling the room with its terrible stench.

The Doc realises his options for rebuttal are few. The road to incredulity is closed. Explanation never had a fighting chance. He stares hard at the weave in the linen tablecloth and says the prayer of all accused men and women –

How do I get out of this?

And a voice he has heard before says back to him –

Give 'em what they want.

He lifts his eyes from the tablecloth and looks hard at both his parents.

"You think me and Duke are homos?"

Mrs Feely puts a hand to her mouth to muffle a reflexive cry to the Almighty. She winced at 'faggot shit', but 'homos', and from her son's own lips, cuts right to the quick of her. Mr Feely, beyond speech, his eyes fixed and staring, his mouth clenched against the filth of the world, makes a tiny motion with his head, as if to say 'Are you?' The Doc looks from his mum to his dad, appraising them with unusual and unexpected coolness.

The light in the room is strange. It seems to pulse. He blinks and shakes his head to clear his vision. All of a sudden he understands that his parents' fear might outweigh their rage. He spies their weakness and wants to hurt them. He wants to make them feel ridiculous. He wants to scare them.

"Well," he says, breathing deeply and sighing. "I guess I'm going through a confusing time at the moment ('Jesus!' 'O God.'). It can get real difficult out there, you know? Lotta bad influences. Lotta bad people. Don't know left from right, right from wrong, ass from elbow. Everything's just topsy-turvy, you know?" and now he stands up from his chair, his hands thumping the table for emphasis, his voice rising to a tremulous bombast, the routine taking over.

"Gays are taking over, you know? Teaching in the schools, sitting in the Government, walking down the streets like they own them or something, and don't even talk to me about the TV, spreading their sick filth on the airwaves. And what can you do, tell me that? I mean you fantasise about all the right girls, you jerk off to all the right porn, you even try not to look at the cocks when you're jerking off to the porn, but what can you do? You can't avoid the cocks, you know? Mr Monster's staring right at you! It's getting to be a crazy world for a young man trying to find his place, a crazy world let me tell you, and I guess sometimes we all act crazy in this crazy world," and now his eyes are ablaze with demonic light, "I mean I guess sometimes even God acts crazy, you know? And, on that point, where the fuck is God in all this anyway? I mean who's in charge here? FUCK IT, maybe God's gone GAY! Maybe the BIG MAN'S just a BIG FUDGE-PACKER!"

His parent's stare at him and the Doc stares back, only noticing now that he's standing, and that his dad looks smaller than usual. Mr Feely can see that he is being made fun of. And that what he thought was the no-contest winning hand is actually stuffed full of jokers. And that he doesn't really know who this person is. Or what he's capable of.

"Go to your room," says Mr Feely.

The Doc goes, taking the postcard with him.

17

The door flies open and the Doc bursts in, his finger tensed on the trigger of his revolver. The balaclava-ed guy by the window takes a half-second too long to cock his shotgun. The Doc shoots from the hip and catches the agent with a slug through the skull. The whites of his eyes scream silent shock before they wink out. He never saw it coming.

Suddenly the Doc is thrown against the wall, bent double over the hole a bullet has just burrowed through his gut.

There's another agent behind the bed.

He thinks the Doc is down.

Think again.

The Doc fires off several rounds as he slides down the wall, his arms clutching the warm, wet mess of his belly. The agent judders as the lead rips through his torso, and blood spatters the window. He falls to the floor and the bed obscures his bleeding body.

But not his face.

The agent stares past the foot of the bed and up the barrel of the Doc's gun. The Doc sees himself now, back to the wall, legs outstretched, left hand limp by his bleeding side, stone-faced and implacable, about to kill this man he doesn't even know. He could call it in, he supposes. Go the official route. For once avoid excessive force. But the gut-shot's taken it out of him. Getting cold already. He doesn't know how much longer he can hold up this gun arm.

Take 'em with you.

He aims for the bridge of the nose. And squeezes. The back of the agent's head explodes in a mist of red and grey.

Fuck it.

He squeezes the trigger again. And again. And again and again until the clip runs out. Until the agent's face crumbles and there's nothing human left.

The Doc gets to his feet and walks to his black leather executive swivel chair, his games-playing chair, and sits down. He kicks off and takes a little turn.

The room kinescopes past his eyes; his WWF posters, his bookshelf, which now has a big *American Psycho* shaped hole in it...

The room blurs from the tears welling in his eyes. He plants his feet, takes a deep breath and says quietly, "Get a grip, you fucking pussy." He sits for a few minutes, feeling the yawning sadness opening up within him, a sense of complete aloneness that fills his chest and his throat. The feeling of desolation is so richly physical it's almost enjoyable.

What to do, what to do...

He jumps out of the chair and goes over to his dresser and stares at a photograph of a seagull which is taped onto bare plasterboard. The plasterboard is bare because it used to be covered by a mirror. The Doc punched through the mirror one day last summer and the seagull photograph covers the hole his fist made when it carried on through the mirror and out the other side into the plasterboard behind it.

He rips the seagull photograph off the wall. He turns it over and reads the name and address printed on the back, and the date; 28th July, 2002. Five months ago. He tries to remember the girl's face and is surprised to realise that he can't picture her.

She was blonde, he remembers that. She was a whole head shorter than him, even though she wore boots all the time; sexy red faux-snakeskin boots. All the time was one week. And then she went back to New York.

He remembers very clearly that he met her in the Temple Bar pub one night, and that he had introduced himself as Patrick Bateman, and that for the whole night he'd been introducing himself to strange girls under the name of his fictional icon. And that he'd been stuck with the name Patrick for practically the whole week because he'd been terrified to tell her the truth. Then when he finally told her about the Bateman thing she hadn't been pissed off or freaked out. She'd found it 'cute'. She had a few things to say about it, smart things, but she found it 'cute'. He remembers that she said 'cute' a lot, almost too much, like girls on MTV. But he loved it when she said 'cute' because she was usually telling him that he was cute.
He remembers that she bought the seagull photograph from an old smoke hound in Dalkey. He remembers how delighted she was with it – "It's like – Crap Warhol!" she'd said. He didn't know what she meant.

"It's like – this is a shit photograph, right? And I paid money for it, right? He made me pay money for shit art! The guy's a fuckin' genius!"

He remembers that she was two years older than him, and vastly more experienced. He remembers nearly having sex with her, so many times nearly having sex with her, but things just not working out right...

He remembers the pain when she told him she was going back to New York the next day. Remembers telling her that you just don't meet girls like her in Dublin. Remembers her saying "Don't guilt-trip me, Johnny," when he started crying. He wasn't trying to guilt-trip her though. He just thought she'd be around for longer.

But it's so hard to remember her face. He wonders how you can possibly forget a face you kissed thousands of times. The face of your first and only girlfriend.

Later that summer, at a party, a big one in Julian's house, the Doc had scored Laura. She was off and on with Houghton at the time and, in a moment of sublimely female treacherousness, decided to score the person Houghton hated more than anyone else.

She cornered him in the secret bathroom upstairs. The Doc had always had a thing for Laura, which of course she knew, and when she pushed him into the bathroom and started telling him that she'd always thought he was a really good-looking guy and then stuck her tongue in his mouth he had responded enthusiastically. But, whether because he was afraid Houghton would pound the door down, or because he was intimidated by aggressive female sexuality, or because he just wished Laura was someone else, one part of him lacked enthusiasm in a very obvious and incriminating way. And no matter how forcefully he ground his loins against hers, no matter how he fondled her nice, loose breasts and her snaking buttocks, no matter how he fantasised about fucking her in every conceivable position, no matter how he fantasised about fucking other girls in every conceivable position, he just could not get it up. And Laura, accustomed to the flattery of that little lump against her belly when she was scoring a guy, even when she wasn't going to do anything with it (and she wasn't) took the Doc's flaccid state personally. Not that you would have read injured pride in her face when she eventually pushed him away, looked him up and down, sneered and walked off. All the Doc read in that ugly/pretty face was disgust and contempt. She got back with Houghton that night.

The seagull looks pretty big, but it's hard to say for certain because there's nothing in the frame to judge him against. He's standing on top of a stone wall, leaden sea behind him and a snippet of the horizon in the top left corner. His yellow beak is stained at the hooked tip with a blush of red, like blood. His yellow eye looks straight into the lens of the camera. It is a terrible photograph.

He turns it over and reads the New York address, e-mail address and mobile number, enunciating each digit clearly to the empty room. He could call her now, he supposes. Just call her up, nice and casual. No need to make up any special excuse, just call her up and say 'How you doing, Kelly Reinhardt, remember me? The nice Irish boy with the nice Irish name that isn't actually my name but the name of a fictional psychopath I have a bit of a yen for. He's a New York psychopath too, so it's like some kind of connection, you know, the way you're a New York girl and I want to be a New York psychopath.' And then he'd say, 'I don't really, though. That's the thing. Don't tell anyone but… I think you were right when you told me I didn't really want to freak those girls out – girls like you – I think I did just, you know, want them to be nice… I used to anyway… but maybe I forgot about that somewhere along the way and it became something else… I know I didn't want to freak you out… and don't get me wrong, I get a kick out of making stuff up and freaking people out, I get a real kick out of it… but something's changing inside me now and I can't stop thinking about blood and killing and there's this clown in my head… I don't know… anyway, no one wants to listen to me anymore, and I guess I'm feeling kind of low, and even Dookey doesn't want to hang out with me, and he was sort of the last one, and my whole year in school hates my guts and my parents think I'm a fag and so does Dookey, well maybe he doesn't; he's got a tricky sense of humour that way, like he might be making a joke but he's serious at the same time, and sometimes I wonder about myself too. I mean, I'm straight, I know I'm straight, but I don't have any actual, you know, proof. Because... I guess. I mean. I'm a virgin. I don't know if you knew that, maybe you did and were too nice to say anything and you see, the thing is, I could have lost it last night, lost my virginity I mean, with a hooker. I mean, I think I could have fucked her, maybe I couldn't have but I definitely could have gone some of the way, and even that, I just think that if I'd even gone some of the way it would all sort of work out, and I was thinking, like, maybe you could help me out, I mean you said you wanted to sleep with me, that you would've and you really seemed to like me, and I really did like you, and I don't want to be just crude and, you know, 'Fuck me please!', ha-ha, but maybe if I went over I could be, like, your Irish boyfriend. I don't mean to get heavy or anything, but just for a couple of weeks while I get my head together because, you know, there's really no one I can hang out with here at the moment; seriously, there's just no one who wants me around'.

Doogie is sitting on his hunkers at the threshold of the Doc's room, staring earnestly. Earnest is the only way Doogie *can* look. He doesn't look straight at the Doc's face, because Doogie hasn't looked directly into human eyes for a long time.

"Hey, Doogie," says the Doc in a soft voice.

He lowers his open palm to Doogie's level and the dishevelled terrier pads towards him. It's slow progress. Eight pads diagonally left, four pads back, eight to the right, four back, his head bobbing and darting every which way apart from his destination. He eventually raises his muzzle to the tips of the Doc's outstretched fingers. Far above his head he hears soft croons of, "Who's a good Doogie? Who's the bestest Doogie in the whole world?" Doogie sniffs his fingers and the olfactory centres in his scrambled canine brain match the scent with something Doc-shaped.

But not too closely, the Doc hopes, nothing too specific, vague outlines of Master, food-bag, Doogie's best friend – not necessarily the person who fed Doogie whiskey and ginger ale until he threw up blood, not the person who sprayed Doogie with hoses and needle-sharp Super Soakers, who blew bubbles into Doogie's limpid, trusting eyes, booted him across garden and kitchen and living room, pushed him downstairs, terrorised him with bangers every Halloween, who performed relentless Pavlovian experiments on him. The Doc strokes Doogie's head and feels him quivering. Is he happy to receive some token of affection, or is he just too scared to run away?

"Sorry about all that evil shit, Doogie. I didn't mean it, you know. Well maybe I did, but..."

But what?

"You've always been a good Doogie. Not the smartest maybe. Not smart enough to learn any tricks or anything. Except weeing on command. That's a pretty good trick. Bet none of the other Doogies can wee on command. Eh? Who's a good little piss-monster? Who's a good little wee-bag? You are. Yes, you are."

"Talking to the dog now, are you?"

"Fuck off, Tom."

Tom's bloated frame fills the doorway, heavy and effeminate with those wide hips and the furry outline in his Polo sweater of what are rapidly growing into a cracking pair of man-breasts. Tom is absolutely the last of all the dull, humourless cunts the Doc wants in his room right now.

"Do you not have, like, fag friends to talk to?" says Tom. "Or is there no time for chat with all the bumming?"

"Seriously, Tom, you just… you just have to fuck off out of my room. I can't listen to you right now."

Tom takes a step into the room and looks around, as though seeing for the first time all the latent gayness on show.

"You going out? Friday night and all that. Down the George. Maybe you're more of a Front Lounge faggot? A fancy fag, yeah?"

"Get the fuck out of my room, Tom."

"Maybe even the other fags don't want to hang out with you. Yeah," says Tom, stroking his hairless chin, "like an old lady fag, sitting at home talking to his fucked-up dog."

The Doc's hands clench and unclench, not sure what to do with themselves. His face is going red. He's afraid, for the millionth time today, that he might start crying. Doogie walks in small, confused circles between the two brothers, wanting to make a break for the doorway but intimidated by Tom's tree-trunk legs. When the Doc stands Tom makes a little mocking feint backwards without actually moving his feet.

"Whoa there! You're not going to bum me, are you? I know you're a sick-in-the-head pervert now but take it outside the immediate family."

Tom's lips curl, pleased at their wit.

Something bursts inside the Doc. It's like there's been a bulb of fluid inside him, twisting him up from the inside out, and now it bursts and all the fluid rushes to his extremities and floods his brain. His back straightens like a line of cruelty and Tom looks smaller and softer. Weaker. The Doc opens his mouth.

"I wouldn't want to fuck you, Tom. Even if I was queer. Just the sight of those Huge. Saggy. Man-tits would turn a fag straight. I couldn't fuck you, Tom. I can't even eat when you're around, you Obese Loser."

That felt good. That felt very good, spitting venom at this pudgy flabsack. His eyes feel like they're glowing. His voice is the voice of God. Tom stands there, rooted to the spot, cheeks blanching.

"So what are you going to do tonight, Tom? You gonna score some Hot Chicks? What's your secret? Comparing bra-sizes? I mean, girls are always impressed by a Massive Pair. Or do you knock 'em dead with tales from the working world? Bowl 'em over with the story of how no-one else would take on this fat, lazy, stupid, useless sack of tits until Daddy decided you could for your pocket money?

The Ladies Love A Winner!"

They advance on each other. In the heat of the routine the Doc is convinced a good, solid stomach punch will burst Tom like a bag of flour. But that doesn't happen. He snaps his fist into Tom's gut but it doesn't have any effect. That sprawling belly isn't soft at all. It's dense. The Doc barely has time to register that the only damage done is to his own skinny wrist when Tom's forehead lands between his eyes. He hears a crack, probably the bridge of his D&G's, and staggers backwards in a shooting, blinding miasma of sinus shock, bursting black in his eyes.

In the aureole of the black spot Stone Cold Steve Austin glares down at him – *Just land the fat fuck on his ass!* The Doc feints, ducks in and under, hooks his right leg behind Tom's right leg and pushes with his whole body and... nothing. *Like pushing a house.* How can one person weigh so much? And now Tom has him, and all his smothering bulk just irresistibly heaves Doc back, while one amazingly powerful arm flicks his unbalanced right leg into the air. There is a nauseating quarter second of weightlessness as the mass of his leg passes into the mass of his torso. Then gravity takes over. The Doc lands on his coccyx, and hears a splintering crack, like all ten knuckles together, through a loudspeaker. Then a yelp.

Doc screams. This scream has originated in Doogie's vertebrae, travelled through the seat of the Doc's pants, reverberated in the cushion of his buttocks, and shot up his spine like lightening. As he screams his mid-section jack-knifes up in a movement that tries to reverse the fall. As though his body could bounce a second back in time. He doesn't, however, have the leverage to bounce all the way up into a standing position, so he's left in a half-crab; his hands on the floor behind him, and his body arching over and as far away as possible from the broken Doogie. He can feel the tingling indentations of Doogie's vertebrae in his buttocks. He hears Tom muttering, "Aw, bollocks." He hears feet pounding up the stairs. He pushes himself off with one hand and twists himself upright. If he had a knife now it would already be buried in Tom's head. But then his legs buckle and he falls over again, beside his dead dog.

Mr Feely joins his two silent sons and realises he doesn't have to shout.

"Well that's what you get," he says, even toned and apparently vindicated. "That's what you get when you mess around like stupid children." He nods his head severely and then says, "I'll get a bag."

"No."

"I'll take care of him," says the Doc. "I'll tie him up in a bag and leave him in the bin so the cats don't get at him. I'll bury him tomorrow morning." The Doc's voice is calm and considered.

Mr Feely looks from the vacant face of his elder son, to the penitent face of his younger son, to the pitiful bow of his dead dog.

"Fine," he says, and goes back downstairs.

Tom stays a moment longer. He looks at Doogie and then at the Doc. He manages a contemptuous snort, as though to say 'If I knew how easy it'd be to upset you I'd have killed the dog sooner'.

Or maybe not. The Doc has never really believed that Tom has thoughts in the normal way. It doesn't matter anyway.

Tom goes. Which leaves the Doc alone with Doogie.

Doogie's eyes bulge, squeezed to the brink of popping out. A puddling trickle of blood congeals on the carpet beneath his open mouth and his tongue lolls.

18

Tom goes out on the piss.

Mr and Mrs Feely watch TV and turn in a little after midnight.

The Doc plays Quake 3 in his room with the sound turned low.

And all through the house not a creature is stirring, because it's dead.

It's an impressive sight seeing the Doc at play, like Kasparov at the chess board, or Michael Johnson breaking from the fray in the 400 metres. Concentration so pure it becomes a thing in itself, disembodied from the subject, a tangible emanation of sheer focus.

The Doc believes himself to be one of the greatest computer game players in the world. Though these days he spends his money on booze he still finds himself pawing through the racks in newsagents to keep abreast of the latest TV popping games and upcoming hardware; hardware so sophisticated that the naked human eye is unable to fully appreciate the sublime perfection of its graphics engine, and the human mind blinks and shudders before the might of its processing power. He scans the letters pages for boasts of high scores, fastest speeds, greatest number of kills, resolves to beat them and always does. However, despite the advent of internet link-ups, tournaments and conventions, serious game-playing remains an essentially solitary activity. So it would be difficult to either prove or disprove this central tenet of the Doc's self-belief. When it comes to the union of mind and PS2, or PS1 or X-Box or GameCube or Megadrive or Saturn or SNES or NES or Gameboy or Commodore 64 or any other permutation of joypad and graphics engine, the world may or may not have seen his like before, and may or may not see it again. But the world hasn't been looking through the Doc's bedroom window.

Sounds in the room. Soft explosive thuds when a cannon shell obliterates a screaming demon. Heavy breathing and clippy-clop footsteps as the Doc's mercenary alter ego patrols the lonely, oppressive corridors. Two loud bangs from the wall; behind it, Mr Feely's night-time fist. Time to turn off the sound completely.

He walks around the level in silence. The killing is too easy. He leaves his mercenary out in the open and a demon starts eating his face. The screen pulses red. The panicked joypad vibrates in his hands. Before his life bar runs out completely he shoots the demon in the head and runs. He knows the geography of this level as well as he knows his own house. He turns a corner and heads for a low wall, beyond which is a precipitous drop. He jumps. It's not very satisfying. There's no function in the game for a headfirst dive, so the mercenary gives the impression of crumpling onto broken legs. But it's enough to finish him off.

The Doc feels a wave of pity passing over him; pity for the faceless grunt he guides around Quake. In the Doc's mind, the grunt in Quake is the same marooned soldier from the Doom series. He thinks of all those millions of hours the soldier has spent being pushed around technologically sophisticated visions of hell, utterly alone, utterly bereft of purpose other than kill or be killed, mostly just kill for the sake of it. A freefall to oblivion is so clearly the only way out that it seems deliberately sadistic of the game's designers not to have included a dignified suicide option. Face-first, the ground rushing to meet his wide, wide eyes.

My eyes are open, thinks the Doc, unable to recall the source of the line. It was a good movie though.

He turns off the PS2 and the TV and sits in the dark, listening to his dad's snores reverberate through the thin walls. Outside his window the suburbs sleep. Or seem to. There are people in those houses out there, people his own age, and it feels to the Doc like they're all having parties. Or at least they're present at parties, doing party stuff, drinking and smoking and scoring. There are girls at these parties, beautiful girls, girls who will never be as young or as beautiful again, and if they were to meet him they might like him. They might at least like the look of him. But he's in here and they're out there. They won't meet him, and they won't ever know him, and who gives a fuck about them anyway? Boring, bland heads full of the Leaving Cert and college courses and plans for the summer… and if they weren't like that they'd be arty wasters like Duke, who was going to be a poet or a movie-maker or a monk, depending on the colour of his piss… or Fitzer, going to make it as a DJ and a fucking freelance music journalist just because he sits around all day getting stoned and downloading new bands off iTunes… or Bob with his stupid cartoons, who can't wait to sell out to an advertising agency, can't even wait to *retire* from selling out to an advertising agency... or Houghton, who'll inherit his dad's company and talk rugby in Ashtons with the other rich assholes, complaining about poor people who are too stupid to be born rich...

And what about me? What the fuck will I do?

His body heaves and he wants to throw up thick black bile over everyone he knows, just open his mouth and blast them like a fire hose, drown the world in viscous fury.

Duke had said to him one time, when the Doc had worked himself up to a steaming, ranting state: 'get over yourself'. People were always telling you to get over yourself. But what the hell does that mean? How do you get over yourself? Duke had explained the way Duke sometimes explained stuff – he waited until the incident was forgotten and gave the Doc a book to read. It was about a monk. Duke was always reading books about monks, or nuns; he really had a thing about nuns. But this book was about a monk, and this monk was always doing 'supererogatory' stuff. Practically every page he'd do something 'supererogatory'. And the Doc had to ask Duke what it meant because it wasn't the sort of word you could just skip over. It was, like, the most important thing about this monk. And Duke said it was like getting over yourself. The monk would make a decision to do something and then he'd do it, even if he didn't want to or didn't feel like it. Especially if he didn't want to or didn't feel like it. Like he'd have to deliver a letter to the King of Spain and he'd decide to take the most difficult route across the Alps, and walk it barefoot, and he had to do it even though he was tired and freezing and close to death – because he had made a decision to do something, to just get over himself, and he had to do it. Supererogatory – good word. You make a decision and you go for it.

Now, alternatively, you might not go for it. You could always sleep on it. You could take it handy and hope for the best, and maybe in a few days or weeks or months everything would go back to normal. And if you go ahead with what you've decided to do then maybe everything will be utterly changed or even fucked up beyond repair. But sometimes you just have to get over yourself and bleed the beast.

The Doc prepares himself for ninja stealth mode. If his parents wake up he's screwed, whether he's gotten over himself or not. He goes down the stairs in bare feet, spider-stepping on the most secure boards. He freezes on the bottom step and listens. His ears take a moment to adjust to the pounding of his blood – behind the submarine echoes in his head there is only silence. He moves on.

In the kitchen he pulls a knife from the block, a short paring blade. There's the faintest ringing scrape of metal-on-wood but he's certain only he can hear it. He slips the knife blade upwards into the back pocket of his school trousers. Then he slips into the utility room and out the back door.

The night is vast. He stretches out his hands at the unbelievable vastness of the sky and tries to position his fingers so each tip has its own floating star. *Crystal Sky Palace* .... He breathes in the cold air; the same air that sits over the whole vast earth, and he's not afraid of the coldness or the vastness. It's like he could jump to any part of the vast earth, like he can touch it just by thinking about it.

Break on through...

Doogie is in the recycling bin under a thick layer of old newspapers. He fit snugly into the silver, zip-lock freezer bag the Doc found in the cupboard over the fridge. The Doc feels a swell of self-congratulation at this piece of native ingenuity. Despite the gale-force shock he had been thinking clearly up in his room and, moreover, under his dad's fearsome glare, clearly enough to realize that without intervention Doogie's body would soon lose heat. And Doogie would be no good to him if rigor mortis set in.

There is definitely still warmth within the bag. But if he can feel heat, it means that heat is escaping.

With the vacuum sealed creature under one arm he moves, at speed, back into the house. The mechanics of what he has to do tick through his brain and he reaches down to a cupboard and takes out a green Tupperware mixing bowl. Needing at least one free hand he wears the bowl as a hat.

Then up the stairs, displacing his weight into the soundless banisters and away from the creaky boards. At the top of the staircase he lets himself into Tom's room, which is the furthest from his parents' room. He closes the door, stands a moment in darkness and gropes for the switch.

Tom's room stinks. All boys' rooms stink, but Tom is a big boy, and his stink is correspondingly overgrown. The main elements of the nasal assault are sweat, semen and stale Lynx.

Now that he's making a wage, Tom insists on buying DVD's almost every day. He has no taste so he only buys box-sets. There's a box-set of Pacino on top of a box-set of *American Pie* on top of a box-set of *Seinfeld* on top of a box-set of boxing movies. The same approach informs his CD collection – all Greatest Hits and Best Ever in the World Ever. The only area in which Tom is really discriminating is porn, which the Doc knows all about because he steals from

Tom's stash on a regular basis.

He lays the bag of dead dog on the bed and unzips it. The inside of the bag is sweaty, like warm chedder.

Sweaty cheese-dog...

"Who's been a bad Doogie," murmurs the Doc, low and loving. "Doogie done a dookey?"

Doogie shat himself when the Doc fell on him and broke his back. The initial turd splat had been taken care of; scooped up, scrubbed down and disinfected into oblivion. In the Doc's mind, the area would never be truly clean, and if he had been planning to stick around he would have had to cut out the offending circle of carpet. It gave him shivery germ tingles; made him feel shit-smeared all over.

Now there was a fresh problem. Maybe, somehow, he'd overlooked it when he'd put Doogie in the bag, or maybe there'd been a certain amount of ... *relaxing* in the time since then, but Doogie is currently half-way through expelling a second stool. The Doc can't leave his dead friend half-way relieved for all eternity. That would be just too much.

Tom has a pile of tissue boxes on a bedside locker. The Doc rifles a thick wad of man-size Kleenex, all the while whispering, "Who's a messy Doogie? Who's a bad boy?"

With baby-handling fingers he pulls Doogie's hindquarters out of the bag. Removing the turd is like removing the stone from an avocado. No amount of tissues would be sufficient to disguise the sensation of yielding softness mixed with grittiness. Obviously some indigestible kernels in Doogie's diet.

He balls up the turd in the tissues and then... *what to do, what to do...* lays it on Tom's vanity table, like an early Christmas present. He wraps more tissue tightly round his index finger and goes back to Doogie's asshole for a tentative root. Some of his disgust melts away as he senses a wave of maternal care washing over him, up to the first knuckle of his devil's finger in Doogie's anus, performing the necessary evacuations. The tissue he then drops on the floor.

Job done. Fit for the ceremonial rites, my pretty.

Now the knife work. He pulls Doogie's dour little skull to the edge of the bed. Doogie's eyes have recessed and his eyelids are half sunk, giving him a crafty look he never had in life. Two pointy fangs are visible, peeking over the thin liverish strips that pass for Doogie's lips.

The Doc wants the blood to flow cleanly, without getting caught in Doogie's throat fuzz. If he had enough time he'd shave the neck area, but he knows that if he waits much longer the blood will coagulate in Doogie's veins and he'll have to improvise beyond his original plan. And the aesthetics of his plan are too pleasing to radically alter now.

He muses over the positioning of Doogie's forelegs, which are hanging over the edge of the bed. He waggles the little paws thoughtfully. Then he tries to bend the forelegs back onto the bed while Doogie's head hangs off the mattress. Ideally the legs would lie straight back, like a sunbathing crocodile, but Doogie's legs are too rigidly hinged to do that. Unless he breaks them. He places one hand on Doogie's back to stabalise him and tenses his fist round the delicate femur. He bends and tests. He could break the hip alright. But he can't do it.

Fuckitfuckitfuckitfuckitfuckitfuckitfuckitfuckitfuckitfuckitfuckitfuckitfuckitfuckit...

The Doc hauls Doogie from the bed, holding him by the scruff, and jams the paring blade into his neck. He saws furiously, forcing the blade through gristly resistances, feeling the sudden rips and pops all the way up his arm and into his teeth. He pictures his dad cutting through roast chicken. Then he feels the blade stab his left hand, having sliced all the way through to the other side of Doogie's neck. He pulls the knife out; terrified that Doogie's head will fall off, and hoists him aloft by the hind legs. He holds the mixing bowl under the rent in Doogie's throat. Then he patiently decants Doogie into the bowl. The blood oozes slowly and thickly. It takes a long time, even with encouraging shakes and squeezes. In the end there's no more than three or four shots worth of gore; stringy and menstrual in texture.

Without letting go of his charge the Doc elbows aside the duvet on Tom's bed. Then he lays Doogie down on his side, his head resting on the edge of the pillow. No matter how he manoeuvres Doogie's head he can't disguise the loose flaps of the rent in his throat, so he pulls the duvet up to Doogie's ears, leaving just the top of the muzzle and the slitted eyes and the still perky ears visible above the bedclothes. He plants a little kiss on Doogie's forehead.

He casts about for something to paint with. Tom's vanity table overflows with potentially useful rubbish. Sure enough, beneath empty CD cases and dusty ties and letters from credit card companies, he finds a layer of Q-tips. None bear evidence of having been used. Three together should make a good daubing tool.

The blood is like scarlet and black oil paint. But too thick. He tiptoes out of Tom's room and across the landing to the bathroom and runs a dram of hot water into the bowl. It sits on top of the gloopy blood and he has to grind out the clots to get an even mixture.

He dunks his hand into the bowl and smears Doogie's blood all over the sheets.

He can see right down into the drying meaty mess of Doogie's throat. "Who's a good boy? You are. Yes, you're a good Doogie! Look what you did. Who's the best Doogie? Who's the bestest Doogie?"

The light in the room is pulsing strangely and the Doc has been bothered by a single high-pitched note for the past few minutes. He hopes he doesn't have an earache.

Or a brain tumour.

He shakes himself alert and moves smoothly off the bed over to the dresser, bowl of blood in hand, and looks at himself in the mirror.

The light levels in the room seem to fluctuate very rapidly, as though the grid were experiencing minute power surges, and the Doc can't even see his own face properly in the oscillating shadow and glare. Framed in the refection of his bloody scrawl he seems darker and older than he's ever looked before.

He puts the bowl on the dresser and works his bloody hands into his hair, right down to the roots, squishing and clenching for a thorough application. With Tom's fake tortoiseshell comb, the teeth impacted with a flaky icing of old gel, he styles his do into his customary executive lick. His hair is thick enough and black enough not to be noticeably discoloured in the low, still pulsing light. Just slick and syrupy. He admires himself; his face obscure and handsome, the walls behind him alive with pulsing light. He teases his blood soaked fringe.

"That'll get crusty," he says to his reflection, his voice strangely high-pitched and American. He sounded a bit like Jerry Lewis. He stares at his mouth, giggles at this new and ridiculous voice, and wonders sincerely, *Was that me?*

The Doc spins around, feeling someone right at the back of his head. Someone huge. A spectral flash in the window catches his eye mid-spin, glowing dimly in the darkness. He swallows a single gulp of saliva that dries out his entire head. His heart is an engine of noise.

"Look at yourself!" he says, and turns slowly round to face the mirror again. His hair catches the strange light and he sees a halo of hellish red over his face. His face is completely white and frozen in an aspect of mortal terror. His own face is the most terrifying thing he has ever seen.

"How big's your third leg?" he says to himself and laughs, a single, triumphant "Hah!"

The voice is a bit like Jerry Lewis and a bit like Ratzo Rizzo, the Dustin Hoffman character in *Midnight Cowboy.* He knows he's responsible for it; he knows he's 'doing a voice'.

This might be it, he thinks.

"This might be it?" he snaps. "What do you mean this *might* be it? This is it!"

No, wait...

"You always wanted to be crazy. People say the Doc's crazy. Bet they'll believe it now. Look what you did, you crazy fuck!"

He looks at it. He really looks at it. Doogie with his three-quarters-severed head and a bed full of blood.

"You ever wake up in a dream where you've gone and killed a bunch of people," he says to his reflection, scowling as if there's another person there, "only you don't remember killing them? But you know you did. And so does everyone else. Everybody knows. And you can't go back to when before you killed them. You wanna go back and tell yourself not to do it. But you can't. It's too late. The job's done. Where you gonna run?"

I'm doing this, he thinks. *I can stop...*

"I'm doing this," he retorts sarcastically. "Hey, here's a good one for you. Why did the doggy cross the road? He didn't, cos you killed him and cut off his head! Haaa-ha-hahahahah!"

But I didn't kill him.

"That's what you say. I say you did. And you're crazy 'cause you killed him and cut off his head!"

I'm not really crazy.

"You style your hair with dog's blood."

That was true. He stares at the scene and sees it properly, suddenly catching the heavy, meaty, butcher's shop smell.

Something like this makes everything true. Everything and anything.

He couldn't ever deny this scene in front of him. He did this. He couldn't ever deny anything ever again.

This makes everything true.

"What a fucking mess."

Shut up.

It is a fucking mess. There's no way he can clean this up and pretend it never happened. There's blood everywhere. The sheets look like a Jackson Pollock canvas. And the ball of tissue paper has sneakily petalled open to reveal its shitty centre.

He shakes all over and then gives at the knees as his stomach convulses and heaves a substantial pat of vomit onto the floor. He braces himself over the vomit, hands gripping his thighs, trying to control the dry heaves, feeling the sweats coming on and expecting his parents to burst into the room any second now. He waits for the pinprick stars to dissolve from his vision.

Then he stands up straight and sees himself in the window again. His slack, staring face is waxy white and his lips are shiny and livid. His hair is tufting skywards, a shock of red over white.

"Hey there, clown-boy," he says.

The floor yawns and yields, losing substance. If he's not careful he might fall right through it. He can't be here anymore.

"Where you gonna go?" he whispers.

His legs bring him to the doorway. He feels his way with his hands, making sure he doesn't bang against the walls. In the bathroom he washes his hands and his face, cleaning off the blood trails from his cheeks and forehead. He looks at the bowl of dog's blood and an idea occurs to him. In his own bedroom he finds an empty plastic Coke bottle, which he takes into the bathroom and fills with Doogie's blood.

Mr Feely has a closet in the hall for his rarely and never worn suits. The Doc picks out a dark charcoal two-piece, undisturbed in twenty years by the looks of it, and a long black trench coat. He puts everything on in his bedroom with one of his plain white school shirts. The bottle of blood fits neatly into the inside pocket of the trench coat. He completes the ensemble with his hard soled patent leather shoes with the heels and his black leather gloves. It feels essential to be well dressed.

Trying to keep his breathing silent, he creeps downstairs. In the kitchen he goes through his mother's handbags and finds her purse with the weekend allowance. He takes ten fifties.

"Stealing from your poor mother now?"

She'll get over it.

Trembling all over, his mind in splinters, feeling like he's left everything he needs behind, the Doc eases the latch on the front door and steps into the still night air. Then he closes the door.

"Wouldn't want to deal with that in the morning."

I guess you're coming with me then.

"I guess you're coming with me," he says, and laughs.

Doc tip-toes to the front gate, nimbly hops over it so as not to suffer the rusty creak, and walks out to the main road. The click of his heels fills the suburban silence. After a few minutes he spies the bright yellow plate of a taxi coming down the road, and sticks out his thumb.

Xavier College looms before him, silent and monstrous in the night. Over the double doors is a large wooden plaque, decorated with the school shield and the motto of all Jesuit schools; Ad Maiorem Dei Gloriam. For the greater glory of God.

"Think we can do better than that," the Doc says to himself.

He gives the bottle of blood a shake, and takes off a glove.

"More fucking mess," he says to himself, and tips a glob of blood onto his fingers. The double doors are set into a wooden and glass frame shaped like the gable end of a Swiss chalet. There are lots of clean, empty windows to transmit his message to the world. He squints over his raised thumb like a painter considering perspective, counts the windows from left to right, and then starts daubing, whistling the Big Top tune as he works.

Doc stands back from his superwork to absorb its beauty. He imagines a camera shot beginning at his feet and rising up his long black back, and raises his arms in time with the imagined movement. The audience sees the back of his neck fringed with congealed blood, and as his head drops out of the frame we see the dark red letters printed across the front of Xavier College:

ABANDON ALL HOPE YE WHO ENTER HERE.

19

Duke opens his eyes and sees his phone vibrating across the floor-boards. He hates his phone, and glares at it until it rings out. He closes his eyes and tries to escape back into sleep. It starts ringing again.

But what if it's a girl? What if it's Laura? What if she's outside right now, aching to take my penis inside her?

He clambers off his futon and onto the floor, grabs his phone and flips it open, solely because he clings to the one in a billion chance that whatever's on the other end will be better than a wank.

It is not.

"Where is my son?"

"Hello? Sorry, who is this?"

"This is Harold Feely. My son goes to school with you."

"Oh."

"This is. *Duke*. Isn't it?"

"Yes, this is Duke."

"Now look. My son is missing and I think you know where he is."

"Sorry, what? I'm sorry, I'm not following."

"Oh, I think you know what I'm talking about. I think it should be very clear. To you of all people."

"The Doc's gone missing? I mean Jonathon's gone missing?"

"Yes, my son has gone missing."

"And you think I know where he is?"

Duke rubs his face and blinks around his room, half-expecting to see that the Doc is hiding in the vicinity, huddled in the laundry corner, crouching like a bad fairy on the bookshelves. Watching him.

"You know damn well where he is! Now look, I'm on to you and, and, and the things you send my son. I've known for some time; I've known since you came into my home that there was something off about you. You've been whispering to him, *twisting* him with your... *weird* little games and the things you send him, and *now* you know what I'm talking about, *don't* you?"

There is a crackle on the other end of the line. Voices move in and out, *"I'll talk to him, Harold," "He's hiding him, he knows exactly what's going on," "Let me talk to him," "This is just an act!" "Give me the phone, Harold. Harold, give me the phone please."*

A woman's voice comes on the line now, flat with exhaustion but courteous.

"Hello? Hello, is that Duke?"

"Good morning, Mrs Feely."

"Not really, I'm afraid. I'm sorry to call you like this but we, that is Jonathon's father and I found your number and you see... Jonathon's disappeared and we thought you might have heard from him."

"I'm really sorry, Mrs Feely, but I haven't seen him since yesterday after school..."

"Now this is important, Duke." Her voice has the trembling vibrato of someone who has been crying for a long time and is trying very hard not to cry again. "Is there anything you can tell me? Is there anything at all? Did something happen in school yesterday? Was Jonathon acting strangely? Please try and remember; please try and remember anything you can tell me because I don't know what's happening and I don't know where he is..."

And then she starts crying, *I'm sorry, I'm sorry, Oh God, I'm sorry,* blubbering apologies into the phone. Duke tries to formulate some sort of response but he knows he has nothing to say that will comfort her. Then Mr Feely comes back on the line.

"Listen to my wife, you little shit! Listen to what she's going through! I know you know something! HE BUTCHERED HIS OWN DOG! DO YOU HEAR ME?! HE BUTCHERED THE FAMILY PET AND NOW HE'S GONE! WHAT SORT OF PERSON BUTCHERS HIS OWN DOG?! WHERE IS HE? I KNOW YOU KNOW WHERE HE IS! TELL ME-"

And then Duke hangs up.

He lies back on his pillow and tries to think. Clearly everything anticipated for today no longer applies. Okay, thinks Duke, I am the Doc.

I am the Doc and I have killed my dog. I have no one to turn to. I am hated and feared and I am full of hatred and fear. I have nowhere to go. Where do I go?

Mr Feely was onto something when he accused Duke of knowing where the Doc was. Duke has spent enough time with the Doc to have developed very acute internal Doc-sensors. On any normal day he can break down the Doc's interests and obsessions into a fairly accurate hypothetical itinerary. He can imagine the Doc in crisis and he can imagine how the Doc might respond to crisis. Today is not a normal day, and from the sounds of it, last night was definitely not a normal night. But Duke has hunches. His first hunch is that the Doc might have gone to the school. It's what Xavier boys do when they lose the plot; they gravitate towards the true centre of their world.

After showering and dressing he examines himself in the bathroom mirror and feels that something is missing. *A detective needs a detecting hat*, he thinks. Gregg's trilby calls to him from the coat stand in the hall. He won't be happy about Duke taking his snappy headpiece, but for the moment he and Duke's mum are sleeping off last night's free wine. Duke grabs his camcorder from his room, lifts the hat from the coat stand, and sneaks out into the chilly morning.

He goes the long way, up the front drive, because this is the way the Doc always approaches the school. An unpleasant image occurs to him – that of the Doc's lifeless body hanging from the copper beech tree in the centre of the school lawn. He quickens his pace, his mind buzzing with connections.

In the past three years there had been three suicides among students and recent graduates of Xavier. Two had been in the grounds of the school, both hangings; one from the senior rugby posts and one from the copper beech. No half-assed cries-for-help; more like screaming Fuck You's. Fuck You People. Fuck This School. Fuck Your 'Ethos'. The dispossessed of Xavier, and the Doc now counted among them, could never escape the school. The school made them, the school was inside them, the school let them be as weird as they could be. And then sometimes the school bit back. The school had allowed the Doc to become the Doc. For years pupils and teachers had been entertained by him and had wanted to see what he'd come up with next. And now the school had laid down the law. 'We made you and we can unmake you'.

Duke rounds the last conifer lined bend of the drive and the view opens up. The lawn is frosty and misted over. The branches of the copper beech are bare.

So what exactly do I do? he wonders. *Scour the frosted grass for boating shoe prints? Check the undergrowth for fresh spoors?*

In the clear bright of day Duke imagines the Doc stalking the grounds in the dead of night. He is getting very clear signals from his Doc-sensors. He knows the Doc was here. But where did he go from here? Duke can see the Doc walking past the houses he is familiar with, houses he has been to parties in. He can see the Doc peering through windows at people he knows, or the families of people he knows, or creeping round their gardens, peeing on the rosebushes, howling at the moon...

Subject left home in the middle of the night. Subject then proceeded on foot to the grounds of his school. We may safely conjecture that the subject's thoughts were morbid in nature, the subject having earlier in the night murdered his dog. Whether the subject's morbidity was self or other directed remains unknown. Subject most likely visited familiar places in the greater Ranelagh area. Having confronted himself with his pariah status subject would then have sought nourishment and a neutral safehouse and made his way to the city centre. Subject may have availed of transport out of the city but we believe he is most likely biding his time in the area.

He takes out his camcorder and records his progress up the long looping drive, panning from the chapel to the headmaster's residence to the back of the science block. The pented roof of the chapel obscures the main entrance to the school. Then he rounds the corner of the chapel and sees it.

Holy fucking Jesus.

Some of the letters are so misshapen as to be illegible, but Duke knows this line very well. Transfixed, unable to move his feet, he zooms in. It's obviously blood. But the creepiest thing is that the letters have been applied by hand. Duke can almost see him there, intent on the job, splashing gore on his fingers.

He's lost it. He's completely lost it.

A door slams and he lowers the camera and looks to his right. An ancient priest is staring at him from the Jesuit residence thirty metres away. He's one of the many retired teacher-priests who shuffle around Xavier in a trance of ecclesiastical meditation or senile dementia. Duke recognises him, but neither of them knows the other by name. Duke decides it's best to maintain the status quo. He turns back towards the drive and strides briskly away. Then he hears a shouted, "Boy! Come back, boy!" and he starts running.

He runs all the way down the drive and into Ranelagh. Then on into Donnybrook and past the Sak's hotel where he and Doc stole the fire extinguisher. He walks down Burlington Street, home of the happy hooker. Makes his way via Baggot Street to Fitzwilliam Square. Takes in two sides of the Square and then on to Leeson Street. Crosses over to Stephen's Green. In the park he wonders why everyone has so many big paper shopping bags and then he realises it's only two days until Christmas.

Grafton Street is mental with foot traffic so he walks down Dawson. As he threads his way through the pedestrians he does something he knows is strange in a city; he looks up.

In any city, but especially in a city of low buildings like Dublin, there is rarely any reason to look up. It's rarely advisable either. You might bump into things, things like people or lamp-posts or buses. But Duke steps off the path onto the edge of the road and looks up. And, as he sees for possibly the first time all the cornices and balconies and friezes and turrets that are always there but never really noticed, he has this thought –

If the Doc were to do something drastic he wouldn't do it quietly. The Doc would want to draw a crowd.

He walks past Trinity and down Westmoreland Street and across O'Connell Bridge. On the north side of the bridge he steps onto the boardwalk and picks up an Americano from the Café Sol kiosk. The taste of coffee reminds him that he was going to make today a smoking day so he doubles back onto O'Connell Street and buys a ten-pack of Marlboro Lights and a box of matches. He feels more like a proper gumshoe with a steaming cup of coffee in his hand and a cigarette between his lips, even if he does cough on the first drag before he remembers how to inhale.

He ambles up the boardwalk. The river is at low tide. It wends its way between bars of mud and silt and greasy black seaweed. Seagulls wheel and caw above and screech at each other down on the riverbed, fighting over scraps of filth. Duke has heard that there are monstrous eels appearing down at the port. Reportedly they are over six feet long and thicker than a man's leg. They've been breaking the lines of trout and mackerel fishermen. Nobody knows where the eels have come from. They might be one of the strange consequences of global warming and changing sea temperatures. They might be mutants created out of the nuclear soup of Sellafield Power Station across the Irish Sea. Duke thinks the eels have always been there but they've only grown massive in recent times because they've been feeding on the increasingly rich filth that the Liffey drains out of Dublin. He thinks this is why the seagulls are getting bigger every year too.

He stops opposite Zanzibar. It's all shuttered up for the day. He thinks he's standing on the exact spot on the boardwalk the Doc performed his fake dive onto two nights ago.

A violent squawking makes him turn around. Twenty feet up a pair of seagulls are dive-bombing each other. They helicopter for advantage and then the first seagull to gain a height advantage torpedoes the other. They freefall for a second in a hectically semaphoring battle of wings and beaks. An unidentifiable scrap falls from the beak of one of the birds and they both swoop down after it. Duke's eyes follow them down. Duke's eyes meet the Doc's eyes.

He is standing on the other side of the river, wearing a Bateman coat and a Bateman suit. His face is pale and his skin visibly gleams with sweat, even from fifty feet. He smiles at Duke and raises a black, Bateman-gloved hand for a single circular wave.

It's happened, thinks Duke. *The terrible thing has happened.*

Duke takes a step to his left and the Doc mirrors him exactly.

Duke steps to his right and the Doc mimics him again.

The quickest way over the river is the Ha'penny Bridge. The Doc sees Duke looking at the bridge, sees him judging the time it would take to cross it. He puts a finger to his chin and raises his eyebrows like a gameshow host asking the audience if they think contestant number one is up to the challenge.

Does he have what it takes? Does he dare? What do you think, folks?

Duke starts walking to the bridge, one eye on the Doc, who is moving in the same direction. Then the Doc runs across the road and up an alley into Temple Bar.

Duke sprints. He swings himself round a pillar and takes the deep steps of the bridge two at a time, spinning away from the other pedestrians. He jumps over a beggar he sees too late. Curses follow him as he skips down the steps on the other side. He darts into traffic, giving rise to an orchestral tuning-fest of angry horns. He runs under the arch that opens onto Temple Bar Square. Because there aren't many shops the Square is less thickly populated than most of the town but there's no Doc in sight. Duke half-runs, half-skips along the row of tourist pubs. He checks the windows and doorways as he passes them, unable to decide whether or not he actually wants to catch up to the Doc.

He carries on up the cobblestone street. As he passes the entrance to Meeting House Square he hears a shouted "Dookey!"

The Doc gives him another taunting wave from the other side of the Square and sprints for the far entrance. Duke follows him and catches a glimpse of black trench coat flapping around the corner where Eustace Street meets Dame Street. He jogs up to Dame Street, out of breath, and sees that he's been given the slip again. The Doc could have ducked into any number of bars and restaurants.

Duke strolls along Dame Street into the shadow of the monolithic Central Bank. It's still early but there are already a dozen or so Emos and Goths and skater kids hanging around the wheelchair ramp and marble benches in the plaza in front of Central Bank. He sits down beneath the spherical bronze sculpture, certain that the Doc is watching him, and resolves to wait in case he decides to reveal his position again. After ten minutes or so a short Emo girl of indeterminable age, shape or attractiveness slopes over to him and asks if he knows where she can buy some hash. He shakes his head. She squints at him reproachfully, apparently convinced that he's holding out on her, then goes back to her friends, shrugging her shoulders. Duke suddenly smacks his forehead and laughs at himself for being such an idiot. He's just realized that he never needed to go looking for the Doc, because the Doc is going to come to him.

The party, he thinks. *He's going to crash the party.*

20

The Doc watches Duke through the window of The Foggy Dew. The pub is dark and empty apart from the Doc and an old-timer at the bar, but chippy frying smells indicate that a lunchtime crowd is expected.

He watches Duke walking around the plaza, watches him searching, pivoting on the spot and whipping his head round like a dancer trying to keep his balance. The Doc wonders if Duke is looking for him or just happened to be in town.

"Wanna bring me in, do ya? Gonna shop me to the pigs, are ya?" he mutters in his clown voice.

The Doc has been worried about the police. He can't break the feeling down into orderable, bite-sized thoughts; he just feels like the heavy hand of the law might land on his shoulder at any second. Or punch him in the back of the head.

The barman is looking down at him with undisguised hostility. Doc goes up to the bar and intends ordering a coffee or a tea but when he opens his mouth he hears himself say, "Bloody Mary!"

The barman winces at the edge in the Doc's voice and says, "Hair of the dog, is it?"

The Doc bursts out laughing and says, "Hair of the dog, head of the dog, and all the rest of him!" The barman laughs uneasily, says, "Right you are," and takes refuge in making the cocktail.

At eight o'clock that morning the Doc woke up on a bench on the boardwalk, after an all too brief blackout. The rising sun was careening up the Liffey from Dublin Port and for approximately two seconds Doc thought he was in his living room armchair, and that he had dreamed the events of the previous day and night. Then the sounds of the city came crashing in on him and the remembrance of what he did with Doogie's body gripped his stomach like an icy fist. He rests his hands on the bar, closes his eyes, and whispers, "Work it, work it, work it, work it..."

"That'll be seven fifty," says the barman. The Doc opens his eyes and glares at him. The Bloody Mary is at his hand, in a tall fluted glass. Doc hands the barman a fifty, and fights the sudden compulsion to smash the glass on the bar top and shove it in the barman's suspicion clouded face. He takes his change and pulls himself away from the bar top, back to his viewing position. Duke is sitting down underneath the bronze sculpture now.

"Plotting against you," he whispers.

Shut up.

A girl in a My Chemical Romance t-shirt walks up to Duke and starts talking to him.

"Dukey's got a girlfriend, Dukey's got a girlfriend..."

No, he doesn't.

The girl walks off. Then Duke claps his hand to his forehead and laughs.

"He knows where you are!"

He knows where I am!

The Doc expects Duke to look straight at the window of The Foggy Dew. But instead he stands up and walks in the direction away from the pub.

"Off to get the pigs."

The Doc sips his drink. Duke keeps walking away and then he crosses the road and heads up Essex Street and out of sight.

"We'll hear the sirens in a few minutes."

Shut up shut up shut up.

He's so very tired. So tired that if he leans his head back and closes his eyes for a minute he might just...

He is awoken from he doesn't know how many minutes of slumber by a sharp increase in pub activity. There are people sitting near him, but not too near him, tucking into chips and chicken nuggets. He gets up, feeling the stiffness of his muscles, and goes to the bathroom, passing a number of new patrons. They're all stuffing themselves full of warming pub-grub, their shopping bags piled up on seats and under tables. In the bathroom he wonders why there's a mirror above the urinal, and then he realises that he's pissing in a sink.

He comes out of the bathroom. A middle aged couple are sitting in a booth directly ahead of him and he finds himself approaching their table. He doesn't know what he's going to do or say even when he's standing over them. The man is heavy set and bull-headed and obviously thinks the Doc is bad news. The woman is a sparky looking forty-something. She raises her face to the Doc. Her eyes are bright with the joy of Christmas shopping.

"Yes?" she says sweetly. "Can we help you with something?"

The Doc stares down at them blankly for a second. Then he

smiles and says, “There’s a clown in my head who wants me to show you my juggling trick.” This line strikes the Doc as the funniest thing he’s ever heard. He laughs so hard he has to grab the couples’ table to keep his balance. His eyes fill with tears. The husband and wife look at each other, anxious and annoyed.

Get a hold of yourself. You’re a professional, dammit.

Then the Doc grabs a handful of chips and sausages off the man’s plate and starts juggling while he doo-doo-doodles the big top tune. As the Doc has no juggling skills and generally poor hand-eye coordination the greasy morsels fly liberally around the pub. Most land on the floor, a few skitter across the tables nearby and one large chip embeds itself in the woman’s perm. The Doc does, however, manage to catch a sausage between his teeth.

The man lunges for him but the Doc leaps beyond his grasp and sprints for the door. He bursts outside, still holding the sausage in his mouth.

21

Duke's mother has decorated since he's been out. On the bureau in the hall there's a small fake tree, decked out in the finest Marks and Spencer's style: boxes the size of sugar cubes wrapped in red foil and tied with miniature golden bows nestling on the nylon branches beside candy canes and hollow bells. There are more festive tokens in the sitting room; a pair of Santa Clause candle-holders on the mantle over the fireplace and a pile of illuminated multi-coloured lights artfully dumped in one corner. Duke's mum has never been troubled by the need of a tree to hang the fairy-lights on. Not that he'd ever tell her but Duke thought this a very admirable quality of his mum's and bitterly resented Gregg's recent rumblings about getting 'a nice spruce for the holidays.'

He climbs the stairs and his legs feel pleasantly wearied from his travels around town. In his bedroom he kicks off his shoes and lies in his bed on his back, listening to Scott Walker's Tilt album. Duke's favourite song on the album is called Farmer in the City.

We're all farmers in the city, thinks Duke. *If only we had something to do with our hands all day we wouldn't have time to go mad. Movies and books and video-games and ideas wouldn't become realer than the world, not if we were in direct contact with it, not if we could feel the earth between our fingers.*

But, he cautions himself, *if we were farmers in the farms, maybe we'd be dreaming of the city.*

Duke closes his eyes and closes his mind to the confusion of it all. In the darkness he sees the Doc in the city, his eyes ablaze, the thresher of his body tearing ragged furrows through the city streets.

22

The Doc runs up Dame Street. The Doc runs up Pearse Street. The Doc runs down to the quays. The Doc crosses and re-crosses the river. He barks directions at himself in the clown voice – "Left! Right! Dead Ahead! Double-back!" Also "Up!" Also "Down!"

He berates himself for not being able to scale the Z-axis.

"It's all X and Y with you, isn't it, you fuckin' fairy? Too pussy to dive. Too pussy to fly."

The Doc isn't a hundred percent on the flying, but it feels like he could fly if he just made the effort. As for the swimming – the Doc doesn't know if he's too pussy to swim or if eventually he'll be too pussy *not* to swim. The urge to jump over the guardrails every time he crosses a bridge is getting stronger and stronger.

On Abbey Street his hand hovers behind a little old lady with a shopping cart who is waiting for a LUAS to pass. The Doc can see the top of a thick stack of Cadbury's Selection Boxes nudging through the top flap of the cart. He comes so close he can smell the old-lady smell of coal-tar soap. His fingers graze the waxy fabric of her old-lady raincoat. He stands a full foot taller than her.

It would take the smallest extension of his arm to push her under the grooved metal wheels. His head is filled with graphic visions of what the wheels would do to the frail old-lady body. The Doc gets so scared he spins around and walks for a mile in the other direction, up past Parnell Square, and through Chinatown and into an estate of flats he's never seen before. He sits on a rusted swing in a broken down playground and takes off his shoes to rub his blistered feet.

A gang of kids mooch into the playground, none of them over twelve, or maybe even ten; the Doc can't tell with kids anymore. They wave sticks at him and shout, 'Pushers out! Pushers out! Kneecap the pushers!' He picks out the kid with the meanest face who seems to be gang leader and tells him that there's a clown in his head who wants him to take the little boy into the burned-out car near the playground and fuck him in the ass. The gang absorb this for a few seconds, adjusting their collective attitude towards the strange sweaty man in the suit who looks like a slightly better-heeled version of the junkies they see every day. Then they start shouting, 'Pedos out! Pedos out! Cut off their willies! Stick em' in their mouth! But when the Doc gets off the swing and takes a few steps towards them they run away.

Eating is problematic. The Doc seems hell-bent on putting himself off his food. He draws unfavourable comparisons between some deli sausage rolls and his own "teeny weeny". A McDonalds burger is a "Splattie-in-a-pattie". The rhymes are nauseating enough on their own but the Doc is also suffering from some extreme synesthesia. When he says "shit" in his clown voice the Doc sees shit and feels shit and smells shit. For the sheer fuck-off-ness of it the Doc buys a kebab from Zaytoons. He taunts himself in a fairly low-key way for starters – "beef-curtains, pork-flaps, lamb-lips" – quickly gets cruder and more literal – "hairy pussy, gonorrhea snatch, droopy cunt, sloppy gash" – imagining that he really is chewing into the living flesh of a woman's crotch. Still he perseveres.

He is half-way through ingesting the kebab when he hears himself say, with a new insidiousness, "Doogie's throat". The Doc looks at the kebab and sees the charnel house of Doogie's throat. He sinks into arterial fissures and past the shocking whiteness of open bone and deep down into the twisted gristle hosepipe of Doogie's oesophagus. Then he throws up the kebab, feeling very sorry for himself, because he doesn't think he'll ever be able to eat again.

The passers-by don't pay him any mind. This is the Christmas season after all, and the Doc could easily pass for just one more young banker out on the tear.

23

Julian lives in one of the big houses on the Ranelagh Main Street, on the same row as the government minister everyone hates, who once upon a time attended Xavier himself. Julian is preparing for the party. He has already made the extravagant purchase of three crates of Stella, three crates of Grolsch, two bottles of Smirnoff and a bottle of Bacardi. If the bastards aren't impressed by that he doesn't know what he has to do. Then he divides what he has by the number of expected guests and realises that there'll only be two bottles of beer and one small shot per drinker. He flies into a steaming, cursing rage; his Frank Sinatra aspirations exposed for the pallid Pop Idol cover versions they always were. He demands more money from his mother, stressing that expectations for this party are sky-high, attempting to barter an increase in party budget in exchange for the Christmas presents she was going to buy him ("But I've already bought your Christmas presents, Julian." "Aagh, Jesus! Birthday presents then! Next years Christmas presents! Work with me here, Mum!") – he prevails by drafting a contract enjoining him to carry out several small painting jobs he was supposed to do last year. When he has the supplementary two hundred euro in his hands he asks her for the eighth time when she's going to Aunt Joan's, "because if you're still poking around when they get here, I swear to God, Mum, I swear to God..."

He makes several more trips to the off-licence. He buys a few cheap bottles of red to make mulled wine but concentrates on increasing the supply of beer. He hopes all this heavy beer-lifting will have some broadening impact on his skinny shoulders. In the mirror in the hall he checks and re-checks his reflection for signs of incipient manliness. Even though he approaches the mirror each time with ever more clenched jaw-muscles and an ever more puffed-out chest, he still looks twelve years old. He shouldn't have let that idiot barber cut his hair so short. It makes him look like he's getting ready for the first day of school.

In the final round robin of text messages he reminds everyone that girls are invited from wherever it is that girls hide out. This is going to be a party to remember, a massive party, a sexy party. There *must* be girls present. Because the last thing Julian wants is another bloody sausage fest.

Fitzer and Steve are in the basement of Fitzer's vast house in Sandymount, the basement Fitzers' parents stopped descending to years back. Steve is jigging about on the couch.

"Hey, Fitzer. Fitzer. Fitzer. Fitzer!"

"What is it Steve?"

"Have you ever heard the ether song?"

"Who's it by?"

"It's by ether! It's what I hear whenever I sniff ether! I bet you do hear it; you just don't know yet. It goes be-doo, be-doo, bom bom, be-doo…"

Fitzer listens benignly to Steve's be-doo-doo-ing his wholly private ether inspired beat.

"That's great Steve," is all he can think to say. "But save some for the party, yeah, man?"

Fitzer stirs the contents of the saucepan in front of him with a fork. According to Fitzer's older brother the best way to prepare magic mushrooms is to boil up as many as possible for as long as possible in a small volume of water. The mushroom season yielded a good crop this year – Fitzer picked over two thousand in a single foraging session around the Wicklow Mountains. The last thousand have been stewing in a litre of water for the past four hours.

The smell is toxic. The water is black and oily like two-day old coffee. Ideally the mixture will be so concentrated that a single, quickly gulped shot will do the trick. Quick enough so that there'll be no need to taste the earthy, musty flavour of magic mushrooms. Fitzer wants tonight to be the ultimate blow-out drugs party. He wants to leave no sense un-deranged. He wants to get as fucked up as possible before he has to enforce a drug sabbatical and get his brain in shape for the Leaving Cert.

No more drugs after tonight, he tells himself.

Except for New Year's Eve, he adds.

And Paddy's Day. Have to get twisted on Paddy's Day.

He nods through the foul-smelling vapours, approving his regime for its realism and sensibleness.

"Steve," he says without turning around, "put the cap back on the bottle."

Fitzer reflects that it's probably a good thing that they've nearly run out of ether. Most drugs had consequential brain damage, but ether's only effect was brain damage. Psychedelics, that's where it's at. Brain expanding, not brain shrivelling. He's hoping the mushroom juice will encourage a real Spirit of '69, Summer of Love style vibe at the party. He's hoping there'll be pretty girls. He's hoping Steve will make a tit of himself in some hilarious fashion. And because Fitzer is a connoisseur of weirdness, and because, despite his mellow, hippyish veneer, Fitzer likes a bit of controversy as much as the next man, he's hoping the Doc will show.

"If he's there tonight, I swear to God, I'll fuckin' destroy him," says Houghton. He drains his can of Dutch Gold and methodically crushes it with one hand.

"It's not like he sent you an actual death *threat*," says Bob, regarding the foolscap page in his hand headed 'Death List'. Truthfully he's relieved that his own name doesn't appear along with Houghton, Laura, Mark and "that pony-tailed cunt from Bob's place," which can only mean Chris.

"I mean, you know it's just his usual pseudo-psycho bollocks," says Bob.

"Maybe it is and maybe it isn't. But he wrote Laura's name there too, and what am I supposed to do about that apart from smash his fuckin' face in?" says Houghton.

"Speaking of Laura," says Bob. "Laura! Can you grab me a beer? Laura?"

"LAURA! Will you grab us some beer?" shouts Houghton.

Laura stomps out of the bathroom where she's making herself up with a friend, stomps into the kitchenette, flings cupboard doors open and shouts back, "I can't find it!"

"It's in the fridge you fucking muppet!" shouts Houghton.

She flings the fridge door open, takes out two frosty cans of Dutch and slams the fridge door hard enough that it bounces open again.

"You left the fridge door open!" shouts Houghton.

"Close it yourself!" she shouts back.

"But that defeats the whole purpose of you getting the beer!"

She dumps the cans in Houghton's lap and stomps back to the bathroom, giving him the finger over her shoulder.

"You guys are a beautiful couple," says Bob.

"Shut up," says Houghton.

A featureless female face, featureless because foundation has been applied according to a blanket philosophy, including lips and eyebrows, peeks into the room. Two startlingly green eyes blink out of the mask.

"Bobby, do you mind if I have one of your beers?" says the face.

"Not at all, darling, help yourself," says Bobby, gallantly indicating the open fridge. The featureless girl totters into the kitchenette. Houghton and Bob appraise her tight little body. She takes a can and blows Bob a kiss then returns to the bathroom to paint her face on.

"What's your one's name again?" says Bob in a low voice.

"Rebecca. No, Rachel, Rachel," says Houghton.

"Tasty. What's she like?"

"Slap addict. Bit of a Mountie. Pure Filth."

"Proper order."

Houghton checks his phone. "Did Chris get back to you?"

"He won't. But he'll turn up if he can figure out the directions," says Bob.

"What do you think of this record producer he's talking to?"

"Complete fantasy. I reckon he downloads his beats off MySpace and then passes them off as his own."

"Seriously?"

"Probably." Bob rubs his belly. "Jesus, I'm wasting away here. Need some proper munch."

They both look over at the kitchen.

"Laura!"

In his flat on South Circular Road Chris practices standing up from his armchair, grabbing his nickel-plated gun and pointing it in the face of whoever might come hammering through the door at any moment. The list of potential intruders is hard to narrow down. Some of them don't even exist. The problem is, which ones?

Chris has been doing coke for about four or five days straight and he's an experienced enough drug user to know that the *intensity* of his paranoia is tied to his massive and sustained cocaine use. That his overriding mental state should be one of paranoia is justified, he feels, by several irreducible facts.

The forces ranged against Chris, the forces that may come knocking at his door, the forces he has determined to meet with maximum aggression are, in no particular order:

1.) His landlady, who left a note informing him that his power will be cut in two days if he doesn't clear out. So far he hasn't had to worry about her because he knows the bitch has never declared on the rental income he gives her, and he's let her know that he knows – but he's between two and three months behind now and his leverage is pretty much gone.

2.) Finnegan, who has already left five messages today. Finnegan is Chris's dealer. A nervy little scumbag who drives around town all day in an Opal Astra with tinted windows and massive exhaust pipes, and who may be afraid of Chris but who may have access to some serious hardcases depending on how much money Chris actually owes him. Chris thinks it's about two grand. Finnegan says it's six. And since Chris dropped his old phone in the jacks two weeks ago he's lost the only records he had of his financial dealings. Without that little electronic ledger Finnegan can make up whatever figures he likes and rely on Chris's memory being a shattered thing of lost weekends and plausible fictions.

3.) His debtors, every last one of them out to screw Chris, every last one of them liable to claim that they're actually a creditor and deserving of drugs on tick, every last one of them liable to claim they're someone other than who Chris thinks they are.

4.) The bank, foremost inventor of those plausible fictions in the form of interest rates on his loan. What started as a ten grand loan over a year ago has somehow only dropped to nine thousand eight hundred, if his memory of the last statement serves, which it probably doesn't.

The flat is another problem. It is alive with filth. His eyes have become skilled at a self-preserving blindness whenever he passes through the kitchen, but his nose has yet to learn the same trick. There's a green thing in the sink which used to be a loaf of bread that is probably the source of the acrid stench but *under no circumstances* is he going to move the baking tray he put there to hide it. He's hoping that fungi and bacteria will battle it out in private until there's nothing left for them to fight over.

He sweeps another pile of burnt down fire log out of the grate and muses darkly on the ash situation. In the beginning he pulled the ash onto the tiled hearth, with the best of intentions to bag it up before things got out of hand. But that time passed and now the ash has spilled over the hearth onto the carpet in a semi-circle extending four feet from the grate, to a median depth of five inches. Everything in the flat has a thin coating of ash. He can feel it in the stiffness of his pony-tail. If he eats in the flat he can taste the grit between his teeth. His suit, his collecting suit, his dealing suit, his 'gangsta' suit, is definitely duller than it used to be. And a man needs to look sharp in this business.

He scrolls through the text messages on his new phone, deleting the messages from Finnegan without looking at them. He has one from Bob and one from Houghton, both reminding him that the Xavier boys are having a house-party this evening. The Xavier boys weren't massive spenders but they nearly always had ready cash and didn't haggle over price. Chris decides that it would be a prudent investment of his time to go to the party. If he catches enough of them out on a wild one he might be able to sort out his immediate cash-flow problems. He might even be able to intimidate a few of them into thinking they already owe him money. The more he thinks about it the more convinced he is that some of them do actually owe him money.

He goes into his bedroom and sorts through his supplies. He still has most of the big block of hash to offload, about two hundred pills and, discounting what he needs for himself, five grams of coke. He turns up the volume on his lap-top speakers. The empty bottles around the room vibrate to the heavy bass. The louder the music the better he feels, and the more manageable his problems seem. If he could just have the music playing this loud all the time he could deal with anything. The world, he decides, needs some sort of device that lets you listen to music at this volume and simultaneously allows you to transact your business with people. The problem with iPods was that you had to keep lowering the volume. The next step for the technology is clearly to make the interface more sophisticated and flexible and... well, let the kids sort out the finer details.

He dances madly around his room, swinging his gun in the air and shooting holes in his problems.

When Duke wakes up from his nap it is dark outside. He turns on his phone. There are three voicemails and a text message from Julian about the party. The first voicemail is Mr Feely, saying, "Hello? Hello?" and hanging up. The next two are from the same number but they play out in silence.

He gets out of bed, feeling a little perverse waking up after darkness has fallen. He takes his second shower of the day and then shaves the wispy fuzz on his chin. After the nap and the shower he feels that he looks refreshed and handsome, and he wonders if Laura will be there tonight, if he'll have anything to say to her. Feeling only the slightest twinge of hypocrisy he splashes on some of Gregg's cologne. Then he rubs in some of his mum's moisturiser to take away the sting.

The house is empty. He potters around the kitchen eating slice after slice of toast and leafing through magazines while waiting for an acceptable hour to go to the party. Anxiety stalks him until half-eight, when he feels he can make a move and arrive at Julian's at a non-loserish hour.

He picks up some cans of Bavaria on the way. He crosses under a LUAS bridge and stops at Julian's driveway, which inclines up to the house. All the windows are bright. He can hear music. Movement is perceptible in the jerk and slide of shadows on the walls and ceilings. Before he walks up the drive he looks up and down the street. To his left, Ranelagh recedes into the suburbs. To the right, the city proper. He scans his Doc-sensor, but the readings are confused. The compass spins freely.

What's he planning? he wonders, and then trudges up the gravel path.

24

The Doc stands on the banks of the Royal Canal. He stares at the reflection of the moon in the still and scummy water. His lips move. Every so often his head shakes violently and he scrunches up his eyelids.

I'd like to stop this now please.

"You can't stop now."

I'd like to go back.

"You can't go back."

I'd like to wake up...

"I'd like to throw up."

What to do, what to do...

"Who to screw, who to screw..."

The clown has this abrasive tic, the Doc has discovered, of rhyming everything. The Doc feels a little deader with every flat and senseless reverberation of his thoughts.

I am the Doc, says the Doc aloud, something he's needed to say more often throughout the day.

"I am the clown".

Have you ever danced with the Doctor in the pale moonlight?

"Let's do the hibbidy-gibbity."

Put on your tap-dancin'...

"Faggot-stompin'..."

Face-stavin'...

"Doogie smashin' shoes!"

The Doc leaves the canal and goes to an off-licence. He buys a half-bottle of vodka, a bottle of Coke and two bottles of Veuve Clicquot. He strides in the vague direction of Ranelagh, holding the bottles by their gilt foil tops.

Flames spark from his shoes. Evil apparitions shimmer over his blood-soaked head.

25

Duke listens out for the peal of the doorbell as he holds his thumb to the brass button and hears someone shouting "Don't ring the doorbell!" Then he notices that the door is on the latch and he pushes it open just in time for Julian's massive hound to reach the top of the basement stairs and rear up on his hind legs like a bear. The dog, a crossbreed wolf/red setter, thumps his forelegs on Duke's shoulders and licks his face. Julian scrambles up the stairs after the hellhound, screaming again, somewhat redundantly, "Don't ring the doorbell!"

The fiery chum breath scorches Duke's nostrils and eyes. Canine tumescence violates his thigh.

"Indy!" shouts Julian in his best school-marm. "Heel!"

Indy has no intention of coming to heel so Julian grabs him by the collar and half-pulls, half-flings him back down the stairs. Duke hears a girlish shriek and a cry of, "Who's a big boy!"

"Sorry about that there, ehh, Duke," says Julian. "He gets worked up by having so many people in the house."

"So long as everyone else gets molested at the gates that's fine by me," says Duke.

"Ehh, yep. Well, you know, make yourself at home, ehh, most people are downstairs and in the garden, ehh, there's beer in the bath, oh you've got your own, that's great, great, ehh, smoking's outside for now, do you smoke? I've forgotten, anyway, outside for now and if it rains I guess we can compromise, not that I expect the bastards to be grateful, I mean it's only my house and I only bought, like, a, a swimming pool's worth of booze for them, which I'm glad to share, you know, don't get me wrong, I'm a generous guy, it's not like I expect, like, ehh, ehh, bowing and scraping or anything. And there's some bagel bites too for, you know. Nibbles."

"That's great, Jules. Thanks for having us over," says Duke, wiping dog slobber from his cheeks and a speck of Julian's spittle from his eye.

"Super, okay, ehh, it's good to see you," says Julian, and then he shakes Duke's hand as though this was a rare reunion and they hadn't been in at least two classes together only yesterday. He precedes Duke down the stairs, muttering about the smell of burning bagel bites.

Duke passes two girls on the stairs he thinks he's met before. He smiles at them cautiously. They smile back with equal caution. Both are quite pretty, if overly made-up and fake tanned, but he opts to leave introductions or re-introductions, as the case may be, to a later and more liquored hour. He heads for the impressive wet-bar Julian has laid out and pours himself a cup of mulled wine to start himself off, thinking, *I am a coward. I am an Irishman.*

He takes his cans to the bathroom and dumps them in the tub, marvelling at the volume of beer in the ice-cubed water. Then he turns around and sees that unopened crates are stacked head-height against the wall.

Enough jungle juice to fuel an army, he thinks, and downs the glass of wine.

Fitzer and Steve turn up bearing drugs. Steve commandeers the piano in the sitting room to hammer out his ether song with some of the musos in the year. Fitzer and Duke get some glasses from the bar.

"You'll only need a shot," says Fitzer, holding forth a 500ml bottle bearing the concentrated juice of a thousand mushrooms. Duke swishes the liquid inside the bottle. He remembers having a nose-bleed when he was eleven or twelve and catching the blood in a test-tube from his junior chemistry kit. After three weeks sitting in his wardrobe the blood looked like this juice.

"Are you sure about this?" he says to Fitzer.

"Why not? It's all natural."

"So is hemlock."

"If you don't want it…" says Fitzer, holding out his hand to take back the bottle.

"Let's not go nuts," says Duke and he pours a measure into a shot glass. He pours another for Fitzer and they clink glasses.

The party really gets going around ten o'clock. Bob turns up with his crew of Houghton, Laura, the Boss and the Boss's pasty-faced sidekick. The League of Gentlemen arrive with a selection of cakes and immediately demand an eating contest. Indy goes bananas trying to mate with Turk, whose own dog is in heat. 'The bitch is in heat!' quickly becomes one of the catchphrases of the night, applicable in nearly any circumstance. Mark turns up and proves an able mouth at the eating contest. Even Ted turns up, and though no one hears him speak there's enough activity that he is able to hang around the fringes without looking out of place. Julian rushes from room to room glad-handing his guests, wrestling his dog from the door, popping up and laughing at jokes he hasn't heard, leaving plates of bagel bites on every available surface, making sure all the girls are introduced to people they already know so he'll be introduced in turn, and generally watching the line of his popularity stock soar into the black. Everyone tells him it's a great party.

Duke challenges Mike Gleeson to a sprint-off in Julian's long and narrow back garden. Gleeson is the fastest runner in the year, a demon on the right-wing for the Senior Cup Team. Duke suspects that a little exercise will speed up his mushroom nausea.

"I coulda been a contender, Gleeson!"

"Think you've got form, Dukey?"

"I AM FORM. Hope you like the taste of dust."

"On three?"

"One-two-GO!"

They belt up the length of the gravel and weed-strewn garden. Duke's cheater's lead is swiftly negated by his spastic noodle legs. He passes the tree that marks the finishing line and throws himself to the ground, ten feet behind Gleeson on a forty yard dash. Gleeson stands over him, not even puffed.

"I could give you a few pointers on your form if you'd like."

"For Christ's sake call an ambulance. Someone put poison in my poison," says Duke between heavy breaths.

Julian's garden ends at a communal alley connecting all the gardens on the row. Sometimes guards patrol the alley because the minister's garden also opens onto the communal area. So when Duke sees two figures standing in the shadows he's momentarily worried that the party is about to be busted. But then he recognises the ponytail and realises its just Houghton and Chris doing a deal. Chris stares daggers at the runners. It strikes Duke as absolutely typical of Chris to seek out the most clandestine area of the grounds to do a deal even though there are drugs all over the house. Several guests have imbibed Fitzer's mushroom juice, Bob has set up a stoner's gallery on the patio, and a bunch of snooty looking chicks from Alexandra College are snorting coke in the kitchen, while Julian flaps around saying, "Easy on the Class-A's guys."

In his own way he's the most pretentious cunt here, thinks Duke, and the thought strikes him like an epiphanyof truth and clarity, and all of a sudden he knows he's tripping. Everything is golden...

"I think Steve's dead!" shouts one of Steve's piano-playing buddies from a first floor window. The garden clears as everyone mills through the basement and up one staircase and the next staircase to the landing where Steve is sitting on the floor, propped up against the wall. His head lolls to one side and his unblinking eyes stare sightlessly ahead. An empty Evian bottle lies by his side.

Amateur diagnosticians crowd around him. One repeatedly clicks his fingers in front of Steve's face. Another holds his wrist and says, "I've got a pulse!" Another takes his limp hand and wafts a lighter under his palm, eliciting no reaction from Steve and announcing, "Irresponsive to stimulus!" A girl holds her make-up mirror to his mouth and says, "It's okay! He's breathing!" Indy lollops through the forest of legs and regards Steve with curiosity. Then he licks Steve's face.

"The dog licked his eyeball! Did you see that?! He licked Steve's eyeball!"

"He's doing it again!"

All watch, transfixed, as the long and liverish tongue scoops the sweat off Steve's purple cheeks and grazes his naked eyeball. Steve's glassy stare never wavers.

"He didn't even blink!"

"Eh, guys, maybe he really is dead. Maybe we should call an ambulance."

Connections are instantly forged between ambulance, cops, and drugs-all-over-the-house. The speaker is drowned out by several vociferous 'No!'s. Fitzer steps in and picks up the empty Evian bottle.

"Too much ether," he says. "He's anaesthetized himself. He's probably aware of what's going on. He just can't move."

He leans in front of Steve and squints through the panes of his eyes at the prisoner of Steve's consciousness.

"You alright in there, buddy? You're just a bit paralysed, okay. You'll be fine in an hour, a couple of hours, max."

All bow to Fitzer's superior knowledge of illicit pharmacological effects. They decide that because Steve is near the upstairs bathroom there'll be plenty of passing traffic to keep an eye on him. Duke, being Duke, stands on the fringes of the crowd, quoting the start of Prufrock to himself –

Let us go then, you and I,
When the evening is spread out against the sky
Like a patient etherised upon a table;

On a bench in Rathmines, with a view of the clock tower, the Doc smokes cigarette after cigarette and takes sips of vodka and cola. The champagne bottles rest by his side. The clock face reads eleven fifteen. He says to the clown, When will you let me go? The Clown whispers back to him, "Not now, not now, not now…"

Laura looks… Laura looks… Laura looks…

Duke can't decide how Laura looks. He turns his head one way and she is radiant; her skin luminous and taut against her cheekbones, her eyes vibrant and blue – and then he turns his head the other way and she is ravaged; that radiant skin suddenly scored and pitted and loose, the eyes dull and rheumy like an old drunk's.

It's the mushrooms, he tells himself, *just the mushrooms.*

She is bobbing her head vaguely to the music. Houghton is nowhere in sight. Duke's feet shimmy across the kitchen floor and he marvels at the lack of stomach butterflies. She pretends to notice him for the first time only when he's right beside her and he nearly laughs in her face at the pretence. But instead he plants a kiss on her cheek, finding it unusually easy to take charge.

"Laura."

"Duke."

"Having fun?"

She shrugs.

"Anything wrong?" he says. "Something up with you and eh-"

"No, no."

Duke hums to himself and is about to walk away when she says, "Do you ever think about killing yourself, Dukey?"

Duke frowns. Morbid thoughts and magic mushrooms do not mix well. But he checks himself for incipient bad trippiness and finds nothing suspect.

"Doesn't everyone?" he says.

"I don't think they do. How would you do it?"

"I wouldn't."

"But if you did. Pills or … what? I think I'd do pills. Some sort of OD."

Duke studies her closely. She's never struck him as the depressive type. Not a real depressive. Duke knows real depressives.

This feels more like attention-seeking.

"So how would you do it?" he hears her say from a vast distance, as though she's trapped inside the Doc's infinite regression of

TV screens.

She's just a girl, he thinks, *she's just a normal, silly teenage girl...*

"Look," he says. "The only thing I know about death is that it'll happen anyway. So you might as well stick around until it does."

He has heard similar things from his dad, and he has said similar things to himself, because everyone *does* think about it.

"But what if life just isn't worth living?" she says.

The cliché is almost too much for him to bear stoically. It seems to Duke that not long ago, maybe not much longer than a couple of hours ago, he'd be gearing up to tell her to leave her boyfriend. But he doesn't want to do that now.

"It's not life that's the problem. It's just... circumstances. Change your circumstances and I'll bet that whatever's making you feel this way will just... disappear."

She's standing closer to him now, not looking at him. He feels the knuckles of her hand grazing the back of his palm. Almost automatically he rests a few fingers on the small of her back.

"Think about this; what if you left Dublin tomorrow and went to... Venice? Really imagine it. And everything that's here stays here. See yourself there in Venice. Would you still be thinking about killing yourself?"

It's a good thing she's not actually looking at him, he realises, because his eyes feel like saucers of lunacy. He tries to blink and can't.

"Maybe you're right," she says and chooses that moment to look into his blasted pupils with practiced seduction. "You make good sense of things, Dukey."

I don't have a crush on you anymore, he wonders, marvelling at his unfathomable nature. *But it would be nice to kiss you all the same...*

Her mouth is close to his. Through the French windows he spies Houghton out in the garden, his head thrown back with laughter.

"I hope I said something useful," he says, leaning down to her ear. "But right now your boyfriend's giving me the evil eye," he lies, and then disengages himself. He suddenly wants to see what else is going on at the party. "Talk later, okay."

He winks at her and bops away to get another beer, thinking, *This is one of those things I realise on mushrooms that I'm supposed to remember later.* He decides he better write it down immediately. Five whole seconds pass before he is distracted by an interesting lampshade and forgets his insight completely.

Julian nods aggressively at a girl who was in last year's musical, concentrating so ferociously at appearing interested and engaged that he has next to no idea what she's talking about. He is stuffing in bagel bites and swigging beer with comparable intensity of purpose, which is unfortunate given that the girl's theme is the eating disorder she has recently overcome.

"...because I'd eat something, something weeshy like a scone, and look at myself in the mirror and I could see the fat piling on. I could see it growing, and I'd say to myself 'I can see the fat piling on,' and I really could, and I could feel my legs getting bigger and my face getting bigger. Like, I thought I had this big fat person's face because I've got slightly chubby cheeks so I'd hold ice-packs to my face for *hours*, you know, so they'd *contract*, and even now I look at myself and think I'm a fattie-fat-fat and I have put on a few pounds, I *have*. I used to be a size four and now I'm an eight or even a ten, realistically, but I'm really learning to love my curves, you know, like Beyonce or Kelly Brook, just love your curves, and I do, most days I do. I do love my curves and it's not the same as being fat, you don't think I'm fat do you?"

Julian keeps nodding and chewing for a second and then adjusts his head movement to a vigorous shake. He says, "Nonononono, not at all, not at all, that's stupid, you're a beautiful girl, really beautiful."

He grabs her arm to reassure her of his honesty and she winces because his hand clamps with excessive and slightly frightening pressure. She gently pats his hand to reassure him that she's reassured and he lets go.

Duke, who has caught the end of her monologue, fixes the girl with his illuminated eyes and says, "You're the most beautiful girl at this party," and then kisses her on the mouth before she knows what's going on. Then he dances away, enormously pleased with himself.

The stunned girl looks from Duke's receding back to Julian to Duke's back.

"What the fuck, like!" she says when Duke is safely out of earshot.

"God, yeah," says Julian, "What an arrogant prick, I'm sorry about that, what an asshole." But he sees the way she keeps glancing in Duke's direction and he also sees the spark of curiosity and excitement in her eyes and he curses himself for not having thought to kiss her first.

What to do, what to do, says the Doc.
"You've just got to be all that you can be", says the Clown.
When am I going to do it, says the Doc.
"Soon, soon, soon," says the Clown.

The League of Gentlemen are twenty minutes into an Hour of Power. Every minute on the minute they've each drained a shot of beer. Benno holds up his arms at forty and waves away the beer-can before his glass is refilled.

"You've gotta hurl!" shouts Turk. "You can only quit if you hurl, Benno!"

Benno burps in the negative and crawls from his chair to a nearby couch for a lie-down.

'Handsome' Brian goes down at forty-three and gamely lurches off to a bathroom. Shayno holds shot forty-five in his bulging cheeks for a few seconds and then sprints for the garden, the bathroom still occupied by Brian. Turk, the last man at the table, downs shot number forty-six and seals victory in fine style. His reward is to chug the contents of a large pewter vase that's been doing the rounds since the game started and is now half-filled with a cocktail of red and white wine, assorted beer dregs, whiskey, vodka, rum and a couple of cigarette butts.

Turk's chugging is a thing of legend. He has no recorded gag reflex and can dislocate his jaw like a snake, which allows him to pour directly to his stomach. The vase, however, is like nothing he's ever chugged before. Turk's internal showman pleads with him to cease this madness, even as his external showman knows he can't resist the steady 'Chug! Chug! Chug!' of the crowd. He lofts the vase for all to marvel at. Then he brings it to his lips, exhales, and pushes the bottom end up. He decants for a solid ten seconds, a few purple dribbles running down his chin, and then collapses in a fit of coughing. He hands the vase to an able assistant, straightens up and smiles at the crowd, a cigarette butt between his teeth. Wild and raucous applause for the conquering hero. The assistant upends the vase to demonstrate that Turk downed the lot. Turk's entire frame shakes violently for a moment, but he gives his audience one last bow and then sits on the floor, head in hands. Minutes later he slumps forward on his face. The crowd agree that he's probably fine. Shortly after, when everyone has adjusted to his prone body being part of the furniture (one girl is using his raised bum as a footstool) he starts vomiting. There's no movement, no convulsions of any kind, his lips just part and a steady flow of multi-hued liquid pours from his mouth.

"Turk's throwing up on the carpet!"

"Ssh! Don't tell Julian!"

"Eew, that is *sooo* gross."

"Look, you can see a face in the vomit!"

"It's Christ!"

"Take a picture!"

"Phone the Weekly World News!"

"That's not Christ," says Michael Nolan. "That's James Joyce."

Heads crane it for closer inspection.

"Oh yeah..."

"Joyce, no doubt about it."

"Who's Joyce?" says one girl with a very high pitched voice.

Michael Nolan is renowned in the year for being the only person to have read *Ulysses* in its entirety. He is utterly incredulous that someone wouldn't know who James Joyce is.

"You don't know who James Joyce is?" he says.

"Nooo," she says, with a rising, taunting inflection.

"He wrote *Ulysses*? The greatest novel of the twentieth century?"

"Well I've never heard of it."

Michael is momentarily struck dumb by the girl's shocking ignorance. Then he points to the door and cries, "Remove the girl!" All the boys in the room join him in demanding the removal of the girl. She giggles at them, knowing that they don't really want to remove her.

"Jimmy Whites," says Chris. "Old-school. Practically pure MDMA. Worth five of the rat turds you get now. Eight quid each. No need to double-drop. Five for thirty."

Bob hands him four twenties for the baggie of pills and an ounce of hash. Rachel said she'd have a pill with him. A single strong pill sounds doable, if he wants to be sure of getting a hard-on later. He suspects he'll end up double-dropping anyway. Chris flicks through the notes and looks at him.

"Yeah, there's that other twenty you owe me," he says.

"Oh yeah?" says Bob,

"Remember I spotted you an eighth off the block the other night?"

Bob does not remember. But that proves nothing and Chris is especially twitchy this evening.

"Oh, right," says Bob, "Fuck, ehh, I've only got another tenner on me, man." He fumbles a dirty tenner out of his wallet and it disappears into Chris's fist.

"Don't sweat it man, you can get me back."

His eyes dart down the garden.

"Here," says Chris, "If you let me have a crack at yer one, we'll call it quits yeah?"

He nods at Rachel, who is sitting on a deck-chair, shivering in her mini-skirt and tiny white jacket. Now that she has a face she is extremely attractive.

"Ah now..." says Bob, hoping this is a joke, knowing it isn't. Bob has his back to a wall and Chris is leaning against the wall, one hand pressed to the mossy bricks behind Bob's right shoulder. Chris's jacket hangs open on his right side and Bob can see the butt of the pistol poking out of the inside pocket.

"Ah *now* what?" says Chris, attempting a chummy smile, which doesn't work because his face is weirdly rigid.

"It's just, you know, it's not really like that..."

"What's it like?"

Bob swallows and flicks his head to the side in a manner he hopes looks nonchalant.

"Well, she's like... she's fair game for now, like."

"So you don't mind..."

"Naw, naw, naw, it's a fuckin' party, man. May the best man win, right?"

Chris gives him a wink and a pat on the shoulder.

"Wish me luck, yeah?" says Chris as he makes for Rachel with his gunslinger's walk.

Bob laughs a hollow laugh and rolls the hash between his fingers.

Duke and Fitzer are both stretched out flat on deck chairs, side by side beneath the depthless sky. The mushrooms are coming on strong. They have formed a silent partnership because making conversation with anyone who isn't on mushrooms is no longer a viable option.

Chris walks between their chairs instead of around them, because he can't pass up on an opportunity to loom obnoxiously. He feints a punch at Fitzer's belly, who spasms self-protectively and then scowls after him. Duke cricks his head around and sees Chris sitting next to the pretty girl who came with Bob, Houghton and

Laura. Duke had half a mind to try to chat her up himself before he realised he was incapable of making full sentences. The mushrooms are a steady thrum of waves in his torso. He contracts and expands like the essence of breath. So does everything else. He hears Chris saying, "You must be tired, beautiful, you've been running through my mind all night." Duke can't even snicker.

"Do you ever wonder…" says Fitzer. He trails off, exhausted by the effort of articulation. Duke hears him breathing in, renewing himself for a speech-assault.

"Do you ever just look up at the stars and wonder…" he says in a deliberately wistful tone. Then both of them crack up at his failure even to be facetious.

Through the blur of giggle-tears Duke traces lines from one star to another. He makes triangles and parallelograms and wonky quadrilaterals and hexagons and octogons and other gons. He fills them in and pieces them together like the facets of some almighty jewel…

"Crystal Sky Palace," he breathes. He tries to imagine the Doc star-gazing. "Couldn't be. It couldn't be…"

"What's that man?" says Fitzer.

Duke concentrates, perspiring from the exertion, and tries to order his words as plainly as possible. "The Doc," he says. "The Doc… The Doc… The Doc."

"The Doc?" echoes Fitzer. "Hey, where is the Doc?"

Where is the Doc?

It is suddenly imperative that Duke write this down. He takes out a notepad and pen from one of his duffel pockets and starts scribbling. He manages to write 'Stars. Crystal Sky Pa' and then the pen stops working. Furious with this setback he examines the pen for faults. The ink cartridge is nearly full. He tests the ball-point with a finger and it seems to be rolling without obstruction. He presses it to the paper and gouges madly, in case there are bubbles in the cartridge that need to be worked through. Time passes.

Eventually he realises that he is still flat on his back and trying to write over his head. He had been convinced he was sitting upright and looking down at the page. He wonders if Fitzer noticed his consternation, and decides that if he can't tell up from down then the profundity of his thoughts might be an illusion. He puts the pen and notepad away and looks around him.

He thinks, *Maybe he ain't gonna show.*

The clock tower strikes twelve thirty. The Doc tears the plastic off his third pack of cigarettes. His body feels like it is made of ash and emptiness.

"Boozed-up. Soft bodied. Bellies upturned. Bared to the knife. You are sharp and in control. You have the power. You will do as you're told."

The Doc sees piles of dead bodies. He sees Houghton's face frozen in a mask of death horror. He sees Laura's pretty head skewered through the ears on a giant shish kebab stick beside Bob's head and Mark's head and Dukey's head...

Dukey...

"Spare the Duke and spoil the Doc."

He sees himself diving into an ocean of blood.

"Now's the time."

On the stoop of Julian's house, Graham Macken and Laurie Murphy are holding forth on the pleasures of masturbating on mushrooms to a trio of thrilled and drug-curious nerds.

"It's like, you can just keep goin' at it, for like, weeks..."

"The visuals..."

"It's like you're inside a cunt..."

"Ten cunts..."

"Twenty."

"Infinite Cunt!"

"It's like..."

Laurie's face suddenly glows with inspiration. "It's like the fuckin'. Apocalypse Now of wanks!"

"Four years in the jungle, man!"

"You don't know where I've been, man!"

"I've seen things!"

They explode with laughter, the drug-curious a little nervously, the drugged with abandon. Laurie squints down the driveway.

"Hey," he says, "is that..."

"Fuck," says Macken. "It's him."

The Doc stands at the end of the driveway, champagne bottles hanging in the shadows of his long black coat. He is staring upwards, apparently looking at something over the house. Laurie looks up to try to discern the Doc's eye-line but doesn't see anything.

The Doc starts walking towards them. The group make a collective decision to stand their ground, not knowing why they want to run and hide.

The Doc walks up the steps between them, his roving stare blankly appraising them each in turn, as though he were window-shopping.

"Gentlemen," he says.

"How you doin', Doc?" says Laurie.

The Doc turns his white face to Laurie without replying. He has absolutely no idea how to answer this question.

Laurie draws back unconsciously. When the Doc turns his scalp is suddenly illuminated by the porch-light directly over his head. To Laurie it looks like the Doc's skull has haemorrhaged. Between the hairs his scalp is livid with flakes and scabs of dried blood. The Doc turns back to the front door of Julian's, which is now wedged open, and he notices a little sign sellotaped over the doorbell which reads, 'Do Not Push!' The Doc pushes. He hears a dog barking upstairs. He smiles.

"He asked for it," whispers one geek to another geek.

The dog comes skittering down the stairs, a red streak of fangs and exuberance. He bounds towards the Doc, half-rears ... and then drops to the carpet, growling. He eyes the Doc from beneath twitching brows, not sure what he's looking at.

The Doc's coat makes him appear massive. The champagne bottles are like clubs in his hands. And his scent... So far as Indy can puzzle out his scent, the Doc is a werewolf. The dog-man takes two steps towards him and Indy draws back, hugging the carpet, ready to pounce. Then the Doc squats down, making his blackness smaller and more manageable, and puts the clubs aside. He takes off a glove and holds out an open palm. Indy inches forward, sniffs the hand, sniffs up the length of the Doc's arm, licks his face happily. The Doc sniffs Indy back, tussles the big furry head and rubs the loose flesh of Indy's throat.

"Bet you could write a whole book with this one," he says.

"You're writing a book?" says one of the company at the door.

The Doc turns around and stares at the interlocutor with malevolent suspicion. Then he grabs his champagne bottles and descends to the basement, drawn to the locus of party noise. Indy follows at his heels.

Because Julian's house is only one room deep, the Doc has been seen through the window at the far end of the front hall by people in the garden. Houghton is already clenching his fists and warning Bob that there'll be trouble when Julian intercepts the Doc with a plateful of cold bagel bites.

"How you doing there, ehh, Doc?" says Julian. "Good of you to come, ehh. Hungry?"

The Doc regards the cold and greasy bagel bites without expression and then looks at Julian for a very long time.

"You got any more dog-meat?"

Julian is acutely aware that the Doc is tickling the back of Indy's neck. He heh-hehs uncertainly at the Doc's new character voice, not getting the joke, not even sure there's a joke to get.

"Heh. Yeah. Heh. Ehh, I see you've made friends with Indy. You're one of the first. Most people are frightened of him."

"He's a good Doogie," says the Doc.

"Yeah. Well, ehh, there's lots of beer left, ehh, though I see you've brought some champagne. That's great, heh, special occasion?"

"The special-est."

"Great. Great. Well, just, you know, make yourself at home. Ehh. Yep."

Julian leaves the plate of bagel bites down and scoots out to the garden, then turns around and pats his thigh and says "C'mon, Indy. C'mon." Indy looks doubtfully from Julian to the Doc and then lopes to his real master. Julian tries to hide his relief by acknowledging an imaginary person over the Doc's shoulder and gesticulating apologies to the Doc for abandoning him.

The kitchen is crowded with people, all in a state of advanced intoxication, who look at the Doc and quickly look away before he meets their eyes. He goes over to the bar, sets down his champagne bottles and pours himself a shot of vodka. He rests his gloved hands on the alcohol-sodden tablecloth and closes his eyes.

When do we start?

The Clown starts a drum-roll.

"Hey Doc."

Duke mooches in the open French window near the bar.

"Dukey," says the Doc without opening his eyes or turning his head. "Dookey left me."

Duke's fingers tap out an uncomfortable rhythm on the window-frame. "Yeah," he says. "I was thinking, ehh. Maybe. Maybe we should make another movie soon. What do you think?"

Duke watches the Doc's lips moving, watches him squinting and shaking his head, hears words humming in his throat that Duke can't make out.

Duke has been around the mad before. It's like a smell you can't quite smell, a thickening of the atmosphere around that person. The Doc is steaming with madness.

"Say, Doc," he says. "Are you thinking of putting on a show?"

The Doc finally turns his white face to him and opens his eyes. The bags under his eyes are yellowy-purple. There's a hairline crack in the bridge of his glasses. And through the fine hairs of his widow's peak (and Duke knows this isn't a mushroom hallucination) his scalp is crusted with blood.

"Look at him!" says Houghton to Bob and Laura. They are on the patio watching the Doc talking to Duke.

"In his fuckin' suit and his fuckin'. Coat. Seriously, who the fuck does he think he is?"

"Looks like he brought a couple of bottles of Bolly, though," says Bob. "Peace offering, maybe?"

"Fuck that," says Houghton. "I wouldn't drink his fuckin' champagne. I'd fuckin'... stick it up his arse if he offered. Which he fuckin' won't."

"I don't like that guy," says Laura quietly, and she hooks her arm in Houghton's.

"Who's the suit?" says Chris, who is suddenly standing beside them.

"That's the Doc," says Bob.

"The Doc? The guy who you all spat on?"

Houghton nods.

"Fuckin' cheek turning up, isn't it? Sort that out, Howie," says Chris.

"How'd it go with Rachel, Chris?" says Bob.

Chris pretends not to have heard him for a few seconds then sticks a hand in a jacket pocket. He pulls out a tiny silver spoon heaped with coke, sniffs and says, "Fuckin' dyke anyway."

The Doc sticks a cigarette between his teeth and picks up his champagne bottles again. He points the tip of the cigarette at Duke and says, "Match me, Dukey."

Duke sees that there is a box of matches on the bar. He strikes one and holds it up for the Doc to suck in the flame.

"Thanks buddy," says the Doc. He sidles past Duke into the garden.

"Hey Howie," says the Doc, striding towards the group. Bob gets a closer look at the Doc's face and fades into the background. Laura stands between the twin pillars of Houghton and Chris and glares at the Doc with catty eyes.

"What the fuck are you?" says Chris. "The fuckin'... stockbroker?"

Word spreads around the party that a fight is about to go down between Houghton and the Doc. The garden crowd inch closer. Spectators slyly file out of the house. A few opine that they hope things don't get too messy and ruin the party. But everyone wants to see a good scrap.

"The stockbroker?" says the Doc. "No, no." He smiles wickedly. "I'm in the business we like to call 'Show'."

He laughs, the cigarette dangling from his sticky lower lip.

"Look here, Doc," says Houghton in a voice he tries to keep level and reasonable, though hostility dribbles from his lips like excess saliva. "The fact is; nobody wants you here. Everyone's just having a good time and they don't want you here. So why don't you turn around and go home?"

"Yeah, why don't you fuck off?" says Laura.

The Doc sucks the cigarette back between his teeth and inhales deeply. Smoke pours thickly out of his mouth and nose when he says to Laura, "Don't I know you, pretty eyes?"

She grips Houghton's arm tighter.

"No!" says Houghton, the tendons popping out of his neck. "You don't fuckin' know her! So do as you're told and fuck off!"

"I am doing as I'm told," says the Doc.

"No you're not!" screams Houghton, his face turning purple.

"Hey now, I don't want no trouble, mister," says the Doc, "But you spat in my face," and he draws back his head as though to hock a big loogie, "So I thought I should return the favour."

Houghton reflexively blocks his face with his hand as the Doc's head shoots forward. The cigarette sails harmlessly between Houghton and Laura and fizzles out in a puddle of beer behind them.

"You missed," says Chris.

The Doc crooks an eyebrow at him. Then the champagne corks explode.

One cork dinks Chris on his pointy chin. The other ricochets off Houghton's forehead. The Doc squeezes his thumbs over the bottle openings and directs the twin spumes over both of them, like a statue in a Las Vegas fountain come to life.

All the other rubber-neckers in the garden fall about, pissing themselves at the Doc's sublime showmanship. Indy bounds happily beneath the last droplets of golden foam. Chris and Houghton stand open-mouthed and spluttering, the champagne freezing through their clothes, both of them incensed but paralysed by the crowd's united show of appreciation for the Doc.

Then Laura screams. "HE FUCKIN' BURNT ME! HE BURNT A FUCKIN' HOLE IN MY HAND!"

She holds her arm out at a warped and freakish angle. Houghton grabs her wrist and stares at the singed hole in the centre of her palm. The burn is even redder and angrier looking than when Duke first made it two nights ago.

Now hold on, thinks Duke. *Everyone saw that didn't happen...*

But Laura's screams cut right through the crowd. She fills the night sky with awful, heart-shaking sounds. And the crowd's sympathy turns on a dime.

"Now hold on a second," says Duke. "Laura!"

Laura, without ceasing her wailing, throws Duke a fearsome glare.

Houghton shouts, "Stay out of it, Duke!"

The Doc is genuinely confused. Especially when the hawk-nosed guy with the ponytail places a bony hand on the Doc's sternum and pushes him backwards, roaring at him to try it on with someone his own size.

"But you're clearly much bigger than me," says the Doc, and then he cracks one hefty bottle into Chris's knee and swings the other at the side of his head. Everyone winces at the hollow thud. Chris sprawls on the ground. His jacket falls open and something shiny catches the Doc's eye.

Houghton lunges for the Doc. The Doc drops his bottles and lunges for the gun. The Doc is faster.

He's thinks he's in movies, thinks Duke. *He's thinks he's in a fucking movie...*

"Doc!" he shouts.

"Put the fuckin' gun down," says Houghton.

But the Doc is not going to put down the gun.

"Make for higher ground," he mumbles.

What?

"Make for higher ground."

"What?" says Houghton.

"Crystal Sky Palace..."

"What the fuck are you talking about?! Put the fuckin' gun down!"

The Doc looks up. Then he turns tail and runs for Julian's flat-roofed garage, throws the gun up top and jumps. He's so pumped he hardly notices pulling himself onto the garage roof. He slips the gun into a pocket of his trenchcoat and starts scaling the old cast-iron drain-pipe.

"He's going for the roof!"

"Why's he going for the roof?"

"How do I know? He's crazy, right?"

He gets to the last chunky clasp holding the pipe to the wall, swings one leg onto the roof slates and grapples his way up. The entire crowd holds its breath as he does a shaky tight-rope walker impression across the slates, four stories up above the concrete patio. Then he turns his back to them and picks his way to the apex. He rests a hand on the chimney stack, the moon clear and full in the sky above him, and lowers his head.

This isn't working.

"It's working great!"

This has gone too far.

"It hasn't gone far enough!"

Enough... enough... I have had enough of you all.

"Take 'em out."

The Doc takes the gun from his pocket.

They watch the Doc take the gun from his pocket and peer at it.

He sees the six bullets in their chambers. He shakes his head. I have had enough of being hated.

"Take 'em out."

I have had enough of you.

"Take 'em out."

I have had enough of me...

Though it is a clear night and a still night there is a breeze blowing up on the roof. It fills the Doc's coat. He feels it pushing him to the edge.

This has to end.

"This *is* the end."

They watch him turn and stride down the slope of the roof. Everyone waits for the skitter of his heels, the loose slate, the death fall.

He looks down at all the upturned faces.

"I suppose you're all wondering why I asked you here today," says the Doc.

One person titters. Chris stirs from his concussion.

"There's a clown in my head who wants me to kill you all."

The Doc aims the gun at Houghton. He pulls back the hammer. The wind makes his coat flutter about his ankles. Above his head, beneath the stars, seagulls wheel and caw. Houghton stares defiantly up at the Doc, stares into the tiny black hole of the gun barrel, feels it like heat on his face.

Time slows down for Duke. Literally slows down as his brain kicks into hyper-speed. He sees everything.

He sees the Doc, a one-man battleground of characters and forces and bits and pieces of personality, all struggling for supremacy, all trying to tear him apart, tearing him adrift from any recognisable reality, all combining to make him the unstoppable centre of attention, the madman he always pretended to be. Duke sees that he's trying to control the forces, trying to step back. Duke sees that he doesn't know how.

He sees Houghton, terrified to die, but even more terrified to give ground to the Doc, caught between two kinds of cowardice that are both pretending to be bravery.

He sees Laura, twisted up by some private and petty bitterness and determined to unleash it on the world. He sees her looking at what she helped to create. He sees that whatever the outcome she will not be healed.

And he sees Chris, who has struggled to his feet and is now standing near Duke. He sees Chris looking at the gun and looking away again. He sees Chris biting his lip and shaking his head. And he sees that Chris isn't at all worried about Houghton being shot.

But he is worried.

"Pull the trigger," says the clown through the Doc.

No.

"Blow his brains out."

No.

"It's not a real gun, is it?" says Duke.

Chris looks at him. He can't hide his shock.

"It's a fake, isn't it?"

Chris doesn't need to say anything.

They want me gone.

"Shoot him!"

I want me gone.

"SHOOT HIM!"

I want you gone even more.

"What?"

Just think about how it'll look.

The Doc sees himself from the crowd's perspective, framed in moonlight, the silhouette of his blood and brains fountaining out of the side of his head. He sees the slow head-first fall to the concrete. Hears the crowd gasp.

They watch him move the gun away from Houghton. Watch him raise it to his temple.

"Duke," says Bob, plaintively.

"It's okay Bobby," says Duke. "It's not a real gun. Let it play."

"But you'll die!"

Yes, I will.

"I'll die!"

Yes, you will.

The barrel is deliciously cold against the soft skin of his temple. He hears the seagulls cawing. He hears Indy barking.

"Are you sure?" says Bob.

"Ask Chris," says Duke.

"I am the Doc," says the Doc. "I'm running the show here."

Then he pulls the trigger.

Everyone hears the click.

"Told you," says Duke, giggling and gasping with relief.

Bob looks at Chris with open contempt.

"What?" says Chris.

Bob shakes his head.

"What? I can still fuckin'... pistol-whip people with it."

Bob snorts.

"You're an absolutely useless cunt, Chris," says Bob, in that practised Xavier drawl; a drawl that could condescend royalty.

The Doc examines the gun. He presses a little button on the side of the gun and the spinning chamber pops out. All the bullets are welded to their individual chambers.

"It's a fake, Doc," yells Duke. "It's all a big fake!"

And the Doc feels like he gets it. He doesn't even know what it is exactly but he gets it.

"Hey, Doc!"

Duke is dancing on the spot and pointing at the night sky, the glittering stars.

"Crystal Sky Palace, right?!"

The Doc looks up. He sees the seagulls up there, utterly unperturbed by what's been happening below. He laughs.

"Hey clown," he says. "How are your acrobatics?"

The clown is a big silent question mark. And then the Doc does something that scares the clown right out of his mind.

They watch the Doc toss the gun over the edge. Watch him look up at the sky again. Hear him shout, "AND FOR MY NEXT TRICK!" Watch him take three measured backwards steps, see his face split into the most maniacal grin. Watch him spring forward two steps, watch him leap. They watch him pinwheel clear of the roof, forty feet above the concrete, his coat concertina-ing around him for a split second and then shooting upwards as he falls, as every heart shoots up into every mouth.

26

When the Doc jumps off the roof of Julian's house, when his feet leave the slates, he realises that he is utterly committed to the possibility that he might die. He realises that he has never before entered into the spirit of an action with such complete abandon. He realises that he has abandoned himself, he has abandoned his family, he has abandoned all these people below him, he has abandoned 'the Doc', he has abandoned life. He feels like a struck tuning fork, ringing out one perfect golden note. The golden note reverberates against reality and bounces back to the Doc, a little stick figure suspended forty feet in the air. He hears the note, encoded with the message of the world. The message is: 'I am alive'.

27

The crowd watch the old iron gutter shake as the Doc grabs it with two black-gloved hands. Watch him hang there, looking into a second floor window.

"Was ANYONE recording that?" he screams, "TELL ME SOMEBODY WAS RECORDING THAT!"

No one replies.

Steve wanders the upper floor of Julian's house. He has no idea where he is. He's trying to remember where one finds water in a house. He wants someone to take his brain out of his skull and wash it carefully in distilled water. He turns in a small circle and sees the Doc suspended in the air outside the window. He shuffles over and pushes the bottom half of the window up.

"Hey, Doc."

"Hey, Stevie-boy."

"What are you doin' out there?"

"I could make the obvious joke, I suppose."

"I have no idea what's obvious at the moment."

"'Hanging around?'"

"Oh yeah. That's a good one. Do you need a hand?"

"Just shift to the side a bit there."

Steve moves and the Doc gets a foot on the sill and grapples his way inside.

"Whew." The Doc wipes his face with his hands. "Thanks Stevie. Well. Gotta run."

"Catch you later, Doc."

Everyone in the garden is recovering from the imagined fall to the concrete. They all felt it. They all saw the ground rushing to meet them. They all felt their bones splintering. They all feel like they've cheated death. They all feel sober, and a little older.

They watch Steve letting the Doc in the window. Watch the Doc flying down the stairs.

Duke sprints up from the basement just in time to see the

black blast of the The Doc streaking out the door. Duke follows him down the drive and into Ranelagh.

It's three in the morning the weekend before Christmas. All the lights are on. Yellow-headed taxis zoom past swaying groups of men and women all dolled up to the nines in the latest finery from Ben Sherman and River Island and Pink and Monsoon and Karen Millen, now creased and sweat-stained from one more pre-Christmas booze-up.

Duke runs after his friend through the diaspora of drunks. He runs as fast as he can, the mushrooms still affecting his vision, making trails out of the taxi-lights and street-lamps. The Doc is a shifting mass of shadows at the centre of the tunnel of light. Duke feels like he's in the part of the movie where the car is speeding through a tunnel in a mountain, speeding to the porthole of light at the end of the tunnel, except in negative; dark is light and light is dark.

"Doc!" he shouts. "DOC!"

"Can't stick around and chat, Dookey!" the Doc shouts back. "I've gotta run!"

The Doc, out of sheer exuberance, jumps onto a bin and vaults off it.

"Where are you going, Doc?"

"I have to get outta here, Dookey!"

"But where are you going?"

"I'm finished here, there's nothing left for me here!"

"BUT WHERE ARE YOU GOING?"

"I'm done with being hated!"

"WHERE! ARE! YOU! GOING!"

"Where do you think? FUCKIN' NEW YORK!"

"New York?!"

"New York!"

"Is this a Bateman thing?"

"Fuck Bateman!"

"Why New York?"

"Have to see someone!"

"You comin' back?"

"Maybe!"

"But Doc…"

"Not the Doc anymore!" Just for a second, Duke thinks he sees a flicker of sadness in Doc's eyes. And just for a second, he sees his friend as nothing more than a frightened schoolboy. Then, a second later, the sharpness in his friend's eyes returns, and the Doc crows:

"The Doc is dead!"

The Doc suddenly spins and back-pedals, which Duke takes as an invitation to relax the furious pace. But all the Doc says is: "I'll send you a letter, Dookey. Gotta run."

And then he spins again. He tears lumps out of the pavement, flames rising from the soles of his shoes.

Duke totters along for a few more stumbling steps and then slumps against a bus shelter. Sparks explode in his oxygen-soaked brain. The world is being shaken up inside a glass bauble. Glitter flakes swirl in his vision. He feels the drugs squeezing out his personality, squeezing out everything he recognises as 'Dukey'. He feels like he doesn't know himself. He feels like he might be nobody. He feels like he could be anyone. He wonders if the Doc feels the same way.

The Doc is dead? think the dissipating remains of Dukey's reason.

Further down the street, Jonathon's run slows to a walk, from a walk to a limp. Duke considers going after him, but something in him says that he should let his friend go alone. He watches the silhouette disappear down the darknening street, until there is nothing left.

ACKNOWLEDGMENTS

My family, Peter, Siobahn, Lindsay, Zoe and the great Nora Rice, for their belief and support.

My early readers, to whom this book is dedicated: Jeanne-Marie Ryan, Kevin Power, Luke Sheehan, Ronan Sheehan, David Fleming, John Cronin, Ronan Raferty, Jesse Weaver, Andrew Nolan, Kevin O'Connor and James Fahy.

Faith O'Grady of the Lisa Richards Agency for all her advocacy and encouragement; Mark Buckland, Anneliese Mackintosh, Gill Tasker and all at Cargo Publishing for taking on the book and providing me with such exemplary editorial guidance; and of course, Anna Day and everyone involved in the Dundee International Book Prize.